"You want your story. I want these women off my back...

"Stay in town and agree to being my girlfriend until this story dies down and I'll give you the exclusive you want."

Her eyes widened. "You're serious?"

"Deadly serious," he confirmed. "I want my life back. You need a promotion. This is a win-win for both of us."

She gave a cute wiggle on her stool. "I think you're giving me far too much credit. Why would women care if I'm your girlfriend?"

"I don't think you're giving yourself enough credit." He stared at her parted lips, shining eyes, her slowly building smile, and closed the distance between them, waiting for her to back away. When she didn't, and even leaned in closer, he said, "Trust me, they'd care." He captured her mouth, cupping her warm face, telling himself the whole damn time this was a terrible idea.

* * *

Most Eligible Cowboy by Stacey Kennedy
is part of the Devil's Bluffs series.

Dear Reader,

If you love fast-paced stories, laugh-out-loud moments, heart-squeezing emotion and sizzling chemistry, then you've come to the right place!

Most Eligible Cowboy is my debut for Harlequin Desire, where Adeline Harlow, a brokenhearted journalist, is desperate for a promotion to salvage the pathetic state of her life after her fiancé cheated. Only one thing stands in her way to get her story and her promotion—millionaire rancher Colter Ward.

After Colter was named Texas's Sexiest Bachelor, his life has turned into a circus. To right his world again, and to continue healing from his divorce, he offers Adeline a deal: he'll give her the best story of her life if she'll fake a relationship with him to get the new ladies in town off his back.

But soon, Adeline and Colter begin breaking all their rules, and that's when things in Devil's Bluffs really heat up. I love this couple, and I hope you do too!

To stay up-to-date on upcoming releases and sales, subscribe to my mailing list at www.staceykennedy.com. To stay in touch, follow me on Instagram and TikTok @staceykennedybooks and on Facebook @authorstaceykennedy. I love new friends!

Happy reading!

Stacey

STACEY KENNEDY

—

MOST ELIGIBLE COWBOY

HARLEQUIN

DESIRE

HARLEQUIN®
DESIRE™

Recycling programs
for this product may
not exist in your area.

ISBN-13: 978-1-335-58151-8

Most Eligible Cowboy

Copyright © 2022 by Stacey Kennedy

For questions and comments about the quality of this book, please contact us at CustomerService@Harlequin.com.

Harlequin Enterprises ULC
22 Adelaide St. West, 41st Floor
Toronto, Ontario M5H 4E3, Canada
www.Harlequin.com

Printed in U.S.A.

Stacey Kennedy is a *USA TODAY* bestselling author who writes romances full of heat, heart and happily-ever-afters. Stacey lives with her husband and two children in southwestern Ontario. Most days, you'll find her enjoying the outdoors or venturing into the forest with her horse. Stacey's just as happy curled up indoors, where she writes surrounded by her lazy dogs. She believes that sexy books about hot cowboys can fix any bad day. But wine and chocolate help too.

Books by Stacey Kennedy

Harlequin Desire

Devil's Bluffs

Most Eligible Cowboy

Visit her Author Profile page at Harlequin.com, or www.staceykennedy.com, for more titles.

You can find Stacey Kennedy on Facebook, along with other Harlequin Desire authors, at www.Facebook.com/harlequindesireauthors!

For Dad,
who bravely battled against Parkinson's.

I miss you every single day.

One

"Hey, sugar."

Sitting atop a wooden bar stool, Colter Ward internally groaned at the cloying perfume infusing the air and itching his nose. Before he arrived at the Black Horse, the legendary cowboy bar in Devil's Bluffs, Texas, he'd figured the dirt and grime under his fingernails from a long day working on a cattle ranch, his unwashed hair and filthy clothes reeking of sweat and God knows what else, would keep any sane woman away tonight.

Irritated he was wrong, he chugged back his ice-cold beer to ease the tight muscles across his shoulders, hearing the liquid's glug in the bottle. The crisp, bitter taste rushed down his throat as he met seductive brown eyes belonging to a woman who on any other night would've spiked his attention. "Not interested." He coldly turned his gaze back to the television screen above the wall of liquor bottles, highlighting the latest Professional Bull Riding championship.

Lust simmered in her raspy voice. "Then I'll give you a few minutes to rethink why you should be interested," she said before heading back to her table on the other side of the bar, where her friend waited.

Colter had come to the bar like he did every Friday after work to unwind, not to find a woman to warm his bed. The place was pure country. Wooden stools butted up against a brass foot rail at a higher counter. Photographs of famous country singers, actors and athletes who'd passed through the small town over the years covered the wood paneling on the walls heading down a dingy hallway to restrooms at the end. Peanut shells littered the floors, and bowls of pretzels were scattered on the round tabletops.

"The ladies after you again?" Riggs Evans, the Black Horse's owner, and Colter's lifelong buddy, asked from behind the bar.

One look into Riggs's amused green eyes, and Colter snorted. "They're worse than a heifer protecting her calf from vaccinations." And he had a dozen scars to attest to a cow's viciousness where it came to keeping her calf safe.

Wiping up the condensation Colter's beer left on the counter, Riggs threw his head back and laughed, bouncing the messy jet-black curls atop his head. "I've never known you not to enjoy the ladies' interest."

"These aren't ladies, they're sharks."

Nearly a month ago, Colter's life had been a disaster after his divorce, but at least it was a quiet disaster. Everything changed when an article came out in a gossip blog out of New York City. In their fifty-state bachelor roundup piece, they named him Texas's sexiest bachelor of the year, after a photograph of him saving a calf from a rapid went viral. Ever since then, not only local women were hounding him, but women had started showing up from out of town chasing after Colter—and his family's millions—looking for some cowboy love.

The attention grated on Carter's last nerve. After his divorce, he'd put his focus on his family's ranch to ensure the Ward legacy continued.

For six generations, the Ward family had worked cattle and bred American quarter horses. Since they were old money, many had wanted to marry into the family over the years, but these past few weeks the women had been relentless. They stalked Colter. In public. At home. Even in his dreams. All he wanted was a cold beer and some quiet after a long, hard week. Not hungry women who wanted his dead heart.

He needed to get this story buried. And these women off his back. For good.

"Ah, dammit," Riggs suddenly snapped.

Down the other end of the bar, Willie, more often inebriated than not, was swearing at another patron, who looked ready to throw the old man against the wall.

Riggs sighed at Colter. "Let me know if you need anything else."

"Sure will." Colter picked at the slippery beer label on his bottle as country beats played through the speakers above the bar. Riggs had become a cop after high school, and a detective after that, but he'd retired after working a difficult case. He didn't need Colter's help. Riggs settled the matter quickly, serving both men a free drink and ensuring they sat apart.

Colter took another sip of his beer as a sweet voice next to him said, "I'll take whatever's on tap."

"Coming up," said Riggs, now back at his post, with a smile Colter had seen a thousand times over.

Her voice sounded familiar, but Colter refused to acknowledge her. He was so damn tired of turning down women. He wanted the spotlight put on the ranch, his family, not on himself. He kept his focus on the television screen.

"Colter Ward, right?"

Could he get twenty minutes to himself? Ready to feed her the same line he'd been using for weeks, he faced the woman with the soft voice, ready to unleash his frustration—but he stopped short.

Long waves of strawberry blond hair curtained a round face. Freckles dusted a small nose, and pouty lips had never looked so pink and inviting. Given that she was wearing a thin blouse and long skirt, nothing was left to his imagination. She had a body made for a man's hands—all the right curves in all the right places. Damn. He'd bet she smelled like a lavender field mixed with sunshine. He began rethinking why he didn't want to take a warm, lush woman to his bed tonight.

"Or am I mistaken?" she asked with a smile that snuffed out his thoughts.

Until he remembered she—and any woman—was

currently the enemy. "Listen, I'm sure you're a wonderful woman, but let me make this unboundedly clear to you: I'm not looking for a relationship. I'm recently divorced and paying alimony to my ex-wife, and I've got enough emotional baggage to fill a barn. Believe me, I might have millions, but the hell I'll put you through ain't worth the money."

She lifted a single eyebrow, sliding onto the stool next to him. "Wow. After that gleaming introduction, I can assure you that I'm most definitely not applying for the job." She stuck out her hand. "I'm Adeline Harlow."

Unable to ignore the manners his parents had raised him with, Colter closed his callused hand around her delicate fingers, returning the handshake. "Colter Ward."

She laughed softly. "Yes, I've already told you that I know who you are. Do you not remember me?"

He gave her another look over, reassessing. "I'm afraid I don't. Should I?"

She pulled her hand away, leaving his skin tingling. "I should think so. I babysat your little brother for an entire summer."

He fought back through his hazy memories, and her name came to him. So did two pigtails, crooked teeth, a chubby face and baggy clothes. "Not the Adeline who'd sit on my parents' couch and write in those journals?"

"That's the one." She smiled.

He could hardly believe his eyes. He'd seen many pretty women, but Adeline was something entirely different. Something...*tempting.* "Jesus, you've left me a little speechless here."

She hit him with a smile full of sass. "Guess that's not a bad way to leave the unshakable Colter Ward."

He laughed dryly. "Believe me, Adeline, I'm shakable." Hating how darkly pathetic he sounded, he took another gulp of his beer.

"So, you're actually human after all, hmm?"

Glancing sideways, he held her playful stare. Though behind the mischievousness, he saw what he needed to know. Back in high school, he'd hung with the popular crowd, and Adeline had not. She thought he had it all. She was dead wrong. "Whatever gave you the impression that I wasn't human?"

Her grin widened. "You are Texas's sexiest bachelor, after all."

Damn that article. "Where did you move again?"

"New York City," she answered and then thanked Riggs as he delivered her beer.

As she took a sip, he asked, "I'm still news in New York City? That article came out weeks ago."

She set her beer down on the paper coaster. "What can I say? People love a hot, heroic cowboy."

He liked—probably more than he should have—that she thought he was hot. To shift the subject off himself, he asked, "Have you moved back to town?" From what he remembered, her mother had moved them away after that summer she babysat his brother, Beau, to be closer to family.

"No, I'm just visiting." Her spine bowed before she straightened her back and smiled again. "How's your family?"

"Beau and my mother are great."

"And your dad?"

Coldness sank into Colter's bones. "Five years ago, he was diagnosed with Parkinson's disease. It's progressing fast." Something Colter would never forgive himself for. He should have been there to help his father when he grew weak. Instead, he'd only focused on his crumbling marriage. He refused to fail his family again.

"Oh, I'm so sorry to hear that." Her hand came to his forearm, her warm gaze offering an alluring comfort.

"Thank you. It's been hardest on my mother." The heat from her fingers on his arm chipped away at the ice in his veins. "My dad's been in a wheelchair for a few months now. He's at a nursing home now but comes home often with the help of a nurse."

"Aw, that's hard." She slowly withdrew her hand, reaching for her beer mug again. "Your parents were always so in love, so it's nice that he can come home sometimes."

Yeah, his parents were madly in love. He'd once wanted a love like that for himself. Until he realized that kind of love didn't happen for everyone.

She watched him closely, awareness reaching her kind, honey-colored eyes. "I saw that your family donated to the Parkinson's Federation this year."

The donation had been the largest his family had made yet—$300,000 in his father's name. "Whatever we can do to further research to help cure this cruel disease, we'll do."

She smiled softly. "Your family has always been so generous to our community."

He caught himself staring into her eyes, feeling an odd

sense of nostalgia. Adeline had known the young man he'd once been, before his heart was ripped out. She didn't look at him like he was broken, the way his family did. Hell, even the way Riggs did sometimes. "So, Adeline, if you haven't moved back to town, why are you here?"

"To see you."

"Me?"

She hesitated. Then she hit him with, "I'm actually a journalist. I work for the blog that named you Texas's sexiest bachelor."

He lifted an eyebrow. "You wrote that article about me?"

"No," she said. "But my editor wants a follow-up story, because you've been such a hit with our readers."

"I see," he said, feeling the walls around him slam up. Wanting nothing to do with anyone involved in the blog that had turned his life into a circus, he polished off his beer. "It was good to see you, but I better get going."

"Wait," she said, clamping onto his forearm again.

He looked at that touch burning his arm, then into her widening eyes, which he almost felt like he could get lost in. Never in his life had he wanted to leave and stay in the same place all at once.

"One interview, that's all I'm asking for," she said with big, pleading eyes. "Then you can go back to your life, and I'll go back to mine."

"That article has turned my life into a spectacle. Why would I let you write another one about me?"

She gave him a beaming smile. "Because I'm utterly charming?"

He felt a crack splinter his wall against her. "No."

Her smile widened. "Because I'm a friend of the family?"

"No."

The playfulness faded from her face, replaced by something fierce that wrapped around Colter and yanked him forward. "Because what stands between me and the promotion I've worked my butt off for for years is an exclusive interview with you. Nothing—and I mean *nothing*—will stop me from getting my interview and earning that promotion. So, either you agree now and make this easy, or we spend the next few days playing a game that neither of us wants to play. But in the end, you will give me the interview."

A chemistry he had not felt in a very long time, if ever, burned between them, tasting rich, raw and tangible. "Why do you think you'd win a game we played?"

Her grin sparkled. "Because I never lose."

Colter could forget his own damn name under that smile. "Is that so?" He closed the distance, leaning near, pulled by something that felt warm, familiar and yet brand-new, too. The local women in Devil's Bluffs kept their distance from a man who'd already failed at marriage and clearly was not on the market. For weeks, he'd been running from women from out of town, all to keep his mind focused on the ranch and off the numb ache in his chest, and none had stopped him in his tracks.

Until *her*.

None had him wondering what she'd do if he acted on the heat burning in his gut and dropped his mouth to hers, declaring a challenge of his own.

Until *her*.

What kind of power did this woman possess?

"Yeah, that's so," she responded, heat flooding her gaze. "I know you're used to getting your own way." *Being a Ward son* echoed in the air between them. "But I'm up for a promotion, along with three of my coworkers. All I need to do is prove myself with an article that blows my competition out of the water. I *need* that exclusive, and you're going to give it to me."

Colter chuckled, both at the gall of her and how much he liked it, right as Riggs cleared his throat and said, "Was asked to deliver this to you."

He set the beer down in front of Colter, but Colter never looked away from Adeline's pinkish cheeks. Damn, he wanted to make those cheeks burn darker. "Send it back," Colter said, and Riggs took the beer away.

All the answers Colter had been looking for suddenly landed in his lap. No one was going to leave him alone. Not these women. Not Adeline. Not the gossip blog. Suddenly, things became clear, and he knew the path to regaining control of his life. "You want your story? I want these women off my back. Stay in town and pretend to be my girlfriend until this story dies down, and I'll give you the exclusive you want."

Her eyes widened. "You're serious?"

"Deadly serious," he confirmed. "I want my life back so I can focus on our ranch. You need a promotion. This is a win-win for both of us."

She gave a cute wiggle on her stool, her skin flushing. "I think you're giving me far too much credit. Why would women care if I'm your girlfriend?"

"I don't think you're giving yourself *enough* credit."

He stared at her parted lips, her shining eyes, her slowly building smile, and closed the distance between them, waiting for her to back away. When she didn't and even leaned in closer, he said, "Trust me, they'd care." He captured her mouth, cupping her warm face, telling himself the whole damn time this was a terrible idea.

And yet…*and yet*, at the feel of her sweet, soft lips, he came undone. She tasted like the past, of easier times, happier times, and of uncontrolled passion. While he'd thought earlier she'd smell like lavender and sunshine, he was pleasantly surprised to find she smelled like sugar and spice. Heat flooded his groin as his scruffy cheek caught on the soft strands of her hair. He had no intention of stopping, but when she moaned eagerly, he remembered they weren't alone. He slowly broke the kiss and reveled in the heat simmering in her half-lidded eyes.

"And how will *that* make them care?" she purred.

"Look for yourself." He gestured to the woman who'd sent him the drink. And as she headed for the door, scowling the entire way, with her friend in tow, he added, "Like I said, they'll care."

Adeline watched the door shut behind the women before addressing him again. "No emotion. No intimacy, except for mandatory kissing to keep up the show. And tell the truth only to people you trust."

He inclined his head. "I can handle those rules. Can you?"

"Believe me, I won't get attached," she said.

He wondered why the promotion was so important

to her, that she'd agree to such an insane idea, but he didn't feel it his place to ask. "Do we have a deal, then?"

The side of her mouth curved ever so slightly as she firmly pulled him into her and said against his mouth, "Yeah, cowboy, we've got a deal. You get a girlfriend. I get the exclusive." Her lips met his, and she owned his mouth, obviously proving a point that she could to both of them. Then she was gone, heading for the door.

"I thought you weren't interested in the ladies," Riggs mused.

Colter stared at the door as it shut behind Adeline, trying to catch up on what in the hell had just happened. He'd never done anything this spontaneous in his life, but he was done doing things the usual way and getting nowhere. He wanted the spotlight off him. For good. "I wasn't."

"Ah, so, she's not a shark, then?" Riggs asked with a laugh.

"No. She's…something else entirely."

Two

The tailpipe of an old Ford backfired as Adeline made it out onto Main Street, fighting the fluttery feeling in her belly. Her high heels clicked against the cracked sidewalks, her knees wobbling.

What in the hell was that?

Back when they were in high school, Colter had been the tough, out-of-her-league guy, while she'd been the quiet, shy girl, lost in her journals. He'd also been her biggest crush.

The day the photograph of Colter had landed on her desk and then went viral, she'd known why he'd become an instant hit with women all over the country. Colter was every woman's fantasy of a real-life cowboy. In the photograph, he'd been shirtless, his body stacked with hard muscle and his face devastatingly handsome. His chiseled jawline with its slight scruff, his full, kissable lips, messy chocolate brown hair and his deep, penetrating blue eyes made women swoon.

Her included. Since she was twelve years old.

Passing by a bakery, she caught a whiff of the yeasty bread browning in the ovens, and she shook out her hands, releasing the tension that was bubbling up. He'd kissed her, and, the most shocking bit of all, she'd kissed him back. She'd chalk it up to insanity, but she knew her teenager's heart was currently bursting with joy.

Still.

What in the hell was *that?*

Feeling well on her way to having an out-of-body experience, she sucked in the fresh air that smelled of wildflowers and continued down the two-lane road. When her mother had swiftly moved Adeline away from Devil's Bluffs, they'd traded one wealthy lifestyle for another. While Devil's Bluffs didn't have a Fifth Avenue, it had the Promenade, a historic block in town. Above the lightly trafficked road, lights twinkled over the entire block of trendy local boutiques and art galleries, along with designer shops, chef-driven restaurants, lively bars and wellness and beauty stores. The pedestrians walking down the streets might have worn cowboy boots and hats, but their jeans and shirts came from top designers.

Desperate to get her head back in the game and off that kiss, she tucked herself into the corner of two shops. She dug her cell phone out of her purse and on FaceTime dialed her best friend, Nora Keller.

The moment Nora's sunny hazel eyes appeared on the screen, Adeline felt her world come together again. Blond-haired and beautiful, Nora was the type of pretty that came from within. Her soul was kind and loving, and that brightness shined through her oval face. Adeline wasn't as calm as Nora, and instead of finding the right words, she blurted out, "I kissed Colter. Or, to be more specific, he kissed me and then I kissed him back."

Nora squealed, dropped the phone, sending it crashing to the ground. When Nora's face appeared again, she gaped, incredulous. "How? What? Why?"

"I'm not even sure what happened," Adeline admitted.

Nora blinked rapidly until her surprise faded to a sly smile. "That is not normally how you interview someone."

Adeline barked a laugh, unable to help it. She'd loved Nora since the day she met her, on her first day of tenth grade at her new school in New York City. She'd never felt alone after she had Nora in her life. "No, it's not protocol that I make out with the people I'm interviewing. But it happened. Oh, man, did it happen."

Nora squeezed her eyes shut tight, shook her head and then reopened her shining eyes, her hand on her chest. "Sorry, I'm absorbing this. I need a minute."

"Oh, is this shocking or something?" Adeline mused. "Wonder why that would be. Maybe because just one week ago I broke off my engagement to the man who I thought was my soul mate and now I'm kissing someone else?"

Nora snorted. "Yeah, *that*."

Adeline tipped her head back against the cement wall behind her and heaved a long sigh, expelling the confusion clouding her thoughts. "I don't even know what happened. It's like one minute I was reminding him I used to babysit his younger brother, and the next I was telling him there's nothing I won't do to get this story. Then he said he'd give me the story if I'll be his fake girlfriend to get all the women in town off his back. Then he kissed me to prove that being his girlfriend would benefit him."

"Well, did it?"

"Did it, what?"

"Did it benefit him?"

"It made a woman hitting on him walk away, so I'd say yes."

Nora blinked. Twice.

"Oh my God, say something, Nora," Adeline gasped.

"I don't even know what to say. This is shocking. And so not like you that I'm still processing." She nibbled her lip and then gave a tight smile. "I mean, Colter is absolutely gorgeous, so kissing him couldn't have been bad."

"It wasn't," Adeline said quickly. "It was…"

Nora leaned in until her face filled up the whole screen. "It was *what*?"

"My God, Nora, it was out-of-this-world incredible," Adeline said on a sigh. "I have never, ever had a kiss like that before, not even with Brock." Who, up until one week ago, had been the love of her life, the man she'd given five years to, the one she'd planned on marrying only a month from now—and the man who was cheating with his secretary, Stephanie.

When her boss had offered her a way out of the city for a little break to interview Colter for an exclusive, she'd jumped on the chance. Brock had texted and called, first every hour, now three times a day, but she hadn't answered a single call or text and powered off her phone unless she was using it. She didn't even know what to say—or where her heart sat in all this mess.

"Honestly, it's like I just lived the very thing my teenage self would have died for. I have no idea what to make of that."

Nora's mouth curved. "Maybe you shouldn't make anything out of it. Maybe this mini vacation won't only be about giving your heart a well-deserved healing moment—and getting the promotion you've worked so hard for—maybe it might be the best rebound vacation ever."

Salacious images of Colter kissing her so passionately in other places of her body stole into her mind. She shivered, still feeling him against her tingling lips. "I'm pretty sure my therapist would tell me doing anything like that is a terrible idea."

"Then she's a terrible therapist and should be fired immediately," Nora said seriously. "Incredible sex with a hot cowboy, who also was your biggest crush, sounds like the best way to heal a broken heart to me."

Adeline laughed. Nora had always been the braver, bolder one.

"All right, so tell me, what does being his fake girlfriend entail?" Nora asked, settling back into a chair. The watercolor painting of the New York City skyline behind her indicated she was in her home office, where she worked as a freelance researcher. "And why does he even need you to do that for him?"

Adeline waited for a pedestrian to walk by before she answered, "I guess the article has brought him unwanted attention from money-hungry women, but to be honest, it almost seemed like more than that."

"Oh, yeah, how?"

"He got divorced a year ago." She learned that tidbit from the article that went viral. "It sounded painful. I think maybe he wants to be left alone." She paused to shrug. "I get the feeling there's more going on there, but I'll keep digging until I have those answers."

Nora gave a lopsided grin. "Well, he wanted to be left alone—until he kissed you."

"Not a real kiss, though," Adeline corrected. Though she couldn't imagine what a real kiss would feel like if that one was for show. "I realize this is an insane idea, but I want his story. Dammit, I'm owed this promotion." Years of hard work and long hours had led to this step-up and pay increase. The day Brock broke her heart, she'd made a promise to herself: no longer would she lean on anyone but herself financially. Her life would not change because she'd thrown Brock out of it. She needed that money now more than ever to cover all the expenses she and Brock used to share.

Nora gave a curt nod. "Just get your story and get back to me here, okay?"

"Believe me, I want that just as much as you do. I'll be home before you know."

"Good," Nora said, pushing her shoulders back. "Text me any updates on Colter. Especially the sexy ones."

"If there is any sexy anything to tell you, you will be the first one I call, believe me." Two pedestrians were coming closer. "I'll call you later, okay?"

"Sure. Love you."

"Love you, too. 'Bye."

Feeling more grounded than when she left the bar, Adeline returned her cell phone to her purse. She straightened her shoulders, lifting her head, ready to face Devil's Bluffs again. The Dove Hill Inn was only two blocks away, where she was booked in for a two-week stay.

Ready to soak her feet in a hot bath and write some notes on the one and only Colter Ward, she only got two steps forward before she froze, rooted to the spot on the sidewalk, her heartbeat thundering in her ears. She took in the old, worn plaid jacket, the jeans with the oil stains and the weathered face of the man coming out of Jackson's Hardware. His dark hair was covered by a faded tan-colored Stetson, and his head was bowed, hiding from the world, his shoulders curled with his hands stuffed in his pockets. For a tall man—over six feet—she'd never seen anyone look so small.

The weakest part of her heart could never forget him. *Her father.* Eric Lowe. A perfect stranger.

She'd only learned his name from her mother when she turned sixteen. Nora had helped find a photograph of him online. One picture of him smiling on the website of the mechanic shop he owned in town.

Adeline clutched her arms to her chest, holding in the warmth trying to seep out of her. A million times she'd told herself what she'd do if she saw him again. She'd confront him, demand answers for why he'd refused to acknowledge he had a child.

Now, in the moment, she did the exact opposite. She dived behind the closest bush, eating dirt and cedar needles, watching as he got into his truck.

"Looking for worms?"

At the low, smooth voice, she shot back to her feet with a gasp and met Colter's amused eyes. "I fell," she lied breezily.

His mouth twitched. "Mmm-hmm." His gaze roamed her from head to toe, bringing heat to places that shouldn't be heated by any man so soon after she'd ended her engagement.

Then again, Colter wasn't any man. Now wearing his black cowboy hat, he was the man of her teenage dreams.

For as long as she could remember, she'd watched him from afar at school, swooning over everything he did. Her journals back then were full of entries about him, and she was sure she had scribbled "Adeline Ward" all over them.

When he met her eyes again, he said, "You don't look injured."

"I'm fine." She blushed, brushing dirt off her knees. "Sorry, did you need something?"

He offered her a card. "I realized on my way back to my truck that I hadn't given you my number. I took a guess you were staying at the inn and was on my way there."

"Good guess." She accepted the card. "Thanks. I'll be in touch tomorrow."

A slow-building grin spread across his face as he winked. "I look forward to it, New York."

And as he turned, heading in the opposite direction, her teenage heart combusted.

The wind feathered through the wild grass and crops as Colter rolled up to the stop sign at the all-way stop. Hardy wildflowers hugged the sunbaked two-lane country road deep in the heart of Ward land. Five hundred and sixty thousand acres of prime Texas countryside were home to six lakes, ten thousand Hereford and Angus cattle, and hundreds of American quarter horses. They sold some of the horses after weaning and shipped them throughout North America. Beau trained those with talent for reining before selling or shipping them off to a professional reiner to increase their value. The stallions at Devil's Bluffs Ranch produced talented, stunning horses, and the price tags for an offspring weren't cheap.

He pressed against the gas, the engine a loud rumble as he drove past the edge of the twenty-five thousand acres of the property that were used for the cattle to graze and to raise crops for internal use. The ranch, established in 1854, was now a well-oiled machine, and Colter felt proud of the legacy of the Ward name.

Ten minutes down the road, he passed the driveway leading to his rustic, ranch-style limestone house with distressed wood accents. The home sat atop a hill overlooking the largest lake on Ward land. He carried on down the road, and soon he passed through the wrought iron gates of his brother's two-story sandstone house, with double cherrywood front doors. On the left side of the property was a twenty-horse barn with a black roof.

When Colter parked his white Ford 150 next to Beau's blue Dodge Ram, he spotted Beau working a horse in the round pen. Austin, Beau's five-year-old son, stood on the fence planks with the heels of his cowboy boots hanging off, barely able to see over the railing. His Stetson looked too big for his slender body, but he refused to wear anything smaller. Austin had a strong personality, just like his dad.

As Colter's boot sent a pebble skipping along the driveway, Austin glanced back over his shoulder. He looked nothing like the mother he'd lost. Annie had died suddenly when Austin was only a few months old—a brain aneurysm, the medical examiner had reported. Austin was all Ward, a near-spitting imagine of his father with wise blue eyes, slightly curly brown hair and a mischievous smile.

"Uncle Colter," his nephew exclaimed, soaring off the fence. His cowboy boots kicked up dirt as he charged forward.

Colter caught the kid as he leaped into his arms. "Having a good day, I take it?"

Arms locked around Colter's neck, Austin beamed. "Dad let me ride Big Joe today."

"Big Joe? Wow, buddy, that's a huge horse to ride." Big Joe was also the oldest, laziest, fattest horse on the farm, but all Austin cared about was being upgraded from a pony.

"I rode him like a champ," Austin stated, wiggling out of Colter's arms and returning to his place on the fence.

Another thing Austin got from his dad—a hefty amount of confidence.

Colter chuckled to himself, watching Beau slap a rope against his leg as the chestnut mare trotted around the pen. When Colter returned to Devil's Bluffs after his divorce, he'd took over the cattle side of the business, as his father could no longer work, but Beau had taken to horses from a young age. There was no greater horseman than his brother.

Beau stepped out in front of the mare, raising his arm. The mare turned the opposite direction and carried on in a trot. Colter had always been proud of his younger brother, but never as much as when he gave up on his competitive dreams as a professional reiner to raise his son after Annie passed away.

Life hadn't been easy for Beau. But for Colter, the best part about coming back to Devil's Bluffs was being more involved in his nephew's life.

Colter reached the fence a moment later, where Beau had already latched the lead rope to the horse's halter and called over a farmhand. "Give her a good walk out before hosing her off," he said, handing off the horse.

The farmhand led the horse away, and Beau took off his cowboy hat, wiping at the sweat on his forehead, and approaching the fence. "Beer?" he asked Colter.

"That'll do."

Beau's gaze fell to his son. "Go help Lee with Pumpkin. Listen to what he tells you."

"Okaaaaay," Austin wheezed, taking off running after the farmhand, who then reprimanded the boy for running up behind the mare.

Colter raised his eyebrows. "Pumpkin?"

"Austin named her," Beau explained, heading toward the house.

Colter fell into stride next to his brother, smiling at his nephew, who now walked slowly and carefully. He couldn't think of a better place to raise a son. It sure beat the big city.

When they reached the porch, Colter took a seat in the closest cedar chair, while Beau headed inside.

He returned a moment later, offering him a cold beer. Beau placed a third beer on the top of the porch steps before sitting next to Colter. "What's up?"

A Friday-night beer had been a long-standing tradition of the Ward men after an exhausting workweek. "You'll never believe who I ran into at the Black Horse just now."

"A woman lusting over you." Beau grinned.

"Hilarious." Colter snorted, stretching out his legs. "No, your old babysitter, Adeline Harlow."

"Adeline," Beau said, mulling over her name. Until awareness filled his eyes. "Pigtails. Overalls. That Adeline?"

Colter nodded. "That's the one. She works for that gossip blog that ran the story about me."

Beau gave a low whistle. "I bet that conversation went well."

"It went terrible. Until I realized we could both get what we wanted. I get a fake girlfriend to appear taken and get these women out of town. She gets the story about me to earn a promotion she's after."

Beau raised his eyebrows. "Care to explain all that in greater detail, since not a lick of it made any sense?"

Colter recapped what had happened since he'd looked up and found himself trapped in Adeline's pretty eyes.

Beau finished his sip of beer and then asked, "Should I be worried about you?"

Colter chuckled against the rim of his beer. "Not that I know of. Why?"

"You're single. You're not dead yet. Why are you so against the idea of women wanting to date you that you're arranging a fake relationship—which, by the way, is insane?" His brother leaned back in his chair, crossing his ankles. "Why not have a little fun? You deserve that."

Colter hung his head, guilt weighing him heavily down into his seat. Had he not focused so much on his own pain with his failing marriage, he would have come home sooner. Maybe his father wouldn't have become so frail so fast if he hadn't had to work so hard. "I've got the ranch on my shoulders. I don't have the time or energy for a woman." And he'd already failed at one marriage.

"Now, that's just a damn shame," Beau muttered. He took another long draw of his beer before he continued, "You said Adeline's pretty now?"

Colter nodded. "Gorgeous."

"Hot in a big-city way?"

Colter pondered the question, remembering just how she'd looked in her high heels, but then shrugged. "Fancy, yeah, but there's some small town there, too." He paused, following his brother's gaze as Austin now climbed on a round bale. "But we both know a pretty face can hide a whole lot of ugly."

"Ain't that the truth, brother," Beau agreed, then gestured out to the driveway. "Might want to tell Mom and Dad about this arrangement before news hits the gossip train."

Colter caught sight of the white wheelchair-accessible van stirring up dust on its drive toward the house. They'd purchased the vehicle for his parents a few months ago when his father was struggling to get around and needed to use a wheelchair. Not long after that, they'd hired a full-time nurse to help his mother at home. As each day passed, things became harder for Dad. He couldn't use the bathroom, shower or eat without help now. That's when they knew he had to move to the nursing home for full-time care.

When the van came to a stop near the porch, Colter fought his instinct to go and help the driver, along with the nurse, assist his father out of the van. His father, Grant Ward, did not like the help, so Colter left it up to the nurse, who knew how to deal with headstrong men.

As the nurse wheeled Dad up to the house, Mom's clear blue eyes met Colter's, her shiny gray curls bouncing with her steps. His mother, Beverly, was a beautiful woman, with a smile that could brighten the coldest of days. He rose and trotted down the porch steps, meeting her halfway. He kissed her cheek. "Hi, Mom."

"Hi, boys." She leaned in for Beau's kiss, and then she reached into her purse, taking out a tall cup with a straw.

She cracked the beer and poured it into the cup as Austin came running over. "Grammy," he exclaimed, launching himself at her.

She awkwardly caught him with a laugh. "Hello, my baby. I'm happy to see you, too." In a classic mom move, she kissed the top of his head. "Come on, let's go in and we can watch a movie. I brought cookies."

Austin charged forward up the steps, and his mother handed Colter the cup with the beer inside and followed Austin into the house.

Colter took a seat on the top porch step, with Beau taking the spot on the bottom. No matter how long it took his mother, the driver and the nurse to get Dad here for their Friday-night beer, he always came. Colter was grateful for that. For these little moments he knew would eventually come to an end.

With shaky arms, Dad held out his hand and took the cup. The nurse gave a smile before returning to the driver, giving them privacy.

"Hey, old man," Colter said.

"Who are you calling old?" Dad joked, the straw rattling in the cup as he managed to get it to his lips.

Colter fought against helping, forcing himself to be still.

Loud music erupted from the living room inside from whatever movie his mother had put on as Dad finished his sip. "Update me on the ranch," he said once he released the straw.

"Nothing much to report on my end," Beau replied. "It's been a good, quiet week—lots of great training. We've got a couple of fancy fillies coming up."

Dad gave a firm nod, slowly placing his cup on the side table attached to his wheelchair. His gaze shifted to Colter. "You?"

He nearly told his father about his arrangement with Adeline, intended to quiet his life that had become a circus, until he looked at the haunting darkness in his father's eyes. His father had his own weight to carry now. Nothing mattered above that. Everything else could wait. "Nothing new here, either," he said, as Beau lifted his brows.

"Cattle's all good, then?" Dad asked.

Colter cupped his father's shoulder, and for the first time in his life, he lied to his father. "Yeah, Dad. I'm all good, and so is the cattle."

Three

The next morning, Adeline woke up early and hit the ground sprinting. She'd done her best not to think of Colter or her father, who probably wouldn't even know she was his daughter if he saw her on the street. Instead, she left the inn for the cozy local coffee shop a block away that roasted its beans in-house. They also had a killer caramelized brown sugar and dulce de leche latte. And one of the best cinnamon rolls Adeline had ever tasted.

Sitting in a corner booth, with her earbuds playing soft rock, she'd spent her morning and early afternoon catching up on emails and scouring the internet for what she could find on Colter. Turned out, it wasn't much. He'd received an award from the city of Seattle for an emergency landing he'd done after the helicopter he was flying lost power. He had saved the life of the governor of Washington, who'd been on board. It didn't come as much of a surprise that Colter had become a pilot of some kind. She recalled he'd taken flying lessons for as long as she'd known the Ward family.

By the time she finished her lunch of chicken, quinoa and Tuscan kale salad, she'd learned all she could without talking to the source directly to fill in the pieces. Determined to write a strong piece—not only for the promotion, but to do the Ward family justice, as she'd always been fond of them—she texted Colter, using the phone number on his business card. Hi. It's Adeline. Can I interview you today?

His response came a few minutes later. Dinner tonight at 6, Longhorn Grill?

She'd never heard of the restaurant and guessed it was new. She responded, I'll be there. See you tonight!

Looking forward to it, New York.

Her belly somersaulted at his obvious nickname for her now. Dear Lord, it was like a man had never called her something other than her name before. Didn't help that she could hear the drawl in Colter's low voice, setting off shivers that desperately wanted to become trembles and moans.

Putting a stop to that nonsense, she slammed her laptop shut and headed back to the inn to finish her work for the day. She curled her hair and added some makeup before swapping out her comfortable clothing for a flowy white frock with a ruffled trim and strappy heels more suitable for dinner.

Once she was back on the town, when dinner was still an hour away, she realized the restaurant was across town near the local newspaper's office and decided to make a quick stop before meeting Colter.

The nineteenth-century building housing the *Devil's Bluffs Chronicle* had received a makeover since Adeline had been there last, with fresh paint and new windows. Though, when she opened the door and it creaked in greeting, the sound was wonderfully familiar. Even the dusty smell hadn't changed. Waylon sat behind his desk, deeper wrinkles on his face than she'd remembered, his hair all silver now.

"Oh my goodness, is that Adeline?" His bright blue eyes were just as Adeline remembered—kind.

"Hi, Waylon," she said, shutting the door behind her. "It's so good to see you."

He rose, moving around his desk with a limp that hadn't been there years ago, to wrap Adeline in his warm embrace. She sank into him, holding tight. Waylon was the reason she didn't hate men altogether. He'd showed her what a good man truly was.

When he leaned away, he asked, "Please tell me you've moved back."

"Sorry, but no," she said before releasing him. "I'm only here for a couple weeks."

Waylon cocked his head. "On a job? I follow your articles all the time."

Of course he did. No one had supported her love of writing more than Waylon. She'd done her high school co-op at the newspaper, and she'd loved every minute of her time there. Leaving Waylon had been the hardest part about moving to the big city, but they'd stayed in contact over email throughout the years.

"I'm actually here to interview Colter Ward," she explained. Waylon's posture perked up, and Adeline smiled, knowing she'd come to the right place. Waylon was a great researcher as well as editor. He gathered secrets like he gathered stories—bountifully. "I wondered if you could tell me a bit about what Colter's been doing since I've left town."

"Not much to tell," Waylon said, limping back to his seat. "He married his high school sweetheart, Julia. Left for Seattle, but, like everyone from Devil's Bluffs, he came back." A pause. "Wasn't quite the same guy, though."

Adeline leaned against the desk. "How was he different?"

Waylon paused to consider, tapping a finger against the armrest. "He's quieter now. Like the city broke him. But if you ask me, it was Julia that had a hand in that."

Adeline studied Waylon's pinched expression. Her mentor loved everyone. "You didn't like his ex-wife?" she asked, surprised.

"Not that I didn't like her, but they were different… not meant to be, I'd say." Then his expression shifted, bringing warmth back into his features. "But the big city looks good on you. It didn't break you at all. Look how grown-up you are. You sparkle, Adeline."

"Thanks," she managed. She didn't feel good inside. After the breakup with Brock, she'd felt crushed, confused and, if she were being honest with herself, lost.

On top of that, she didn't feel like she belonged in the big city anymore, as much as she didn't feel like she belonged in Devil's Bluffs.

Just as the room began to close in on her, she hastily shoved thoughts of her life away, staying focused on Colter. "You haven't heard anything more about him from any of the gossip in town?" Small towns, even wealthy towns, always had a long line of gossipers. "Nothing that I might use in my story?"

"Colter is good stuff. Both those Ward boys are. They do a lot for the town and take good care of their parents. If you write anything, write about that."

Adeline took some mental notes, but she knew Colter being a good man wouldn't give her the enticing piece she needed to earn her the promotion. She needed to dig deep, find Colter's truth, his weaknesses, his successes—which would only make him more attractive to the blog's readers.

Waylon's watch beeped, drawing his gaze. "And that's a day." He rose, powered off his computer and gently escorted Adeline out before locking up. She'd always respected Waylon's balance between home and family life. He made time for his wife of forty years and his children. Always.

"It really is so great to see you," Adeline said. "Say hi to Marjorie for me."

"I sure will."

Adeline hugged him once more and said her goodbyes with the promise to come back soon. Though she was getting tidbits of Colter's story, she knew all the good details would come from dinner tonight.

The Longhorn Grill was only a two-minute walk down the moderately busy street, and when she arrived at the chic, modern restaurant with bright white walls and warm wooden accents, a hostess seated her quickly.

Then the front door opened, and Colter entered, speaking to the hostess. Adeline swallowed. Deeply. *I am in way over my head.*

Yesterday, Colter had looked rough, like a cowboy who'd spent his day working hard on the ranch. He'd smelled of sweat, of man and of things that shouldn't arouse a woman, but somehow had only made him more masculine. She exhaled against the quickening of her breath at his crisp black button-up tucked into light jeans that hugged his thick thighs. She'd never felt jealous of clothes before, but she'd give her last year's salary to mold herself to Colter the way the fabric did. Warmth flooded her when his stare caught hers and held as he began walking to the table, the side of his mouth curving. Dear Lord, *that* man was far too handsome for his own good, oozing testosterone and charm, nearly melting her into a puddle on the hardwood floors.

Two women had followed him into the restaurant, but as they saw him headed Adeline's way, they frowned and turned their attention to the two cowboys sitting at the bar. Gosh, the women really were relentless.

When Colter reached the table, he leaned near, and her nerve endings stirred as his lips met hers. The kiss was polite, a show for their audience in the restaurant. Her body forgot that memo, and as he pulled away, she moved with him, reaching for *more*. Light-headed, she inhaled his spicy, woodsy scent and wanted to forget that she'd *just* broken off her engagement and her heart was still raw and bleeding.

Before she crawled up his strong body, she yanked herself back and relaxed her posture, like his kiss didn't send her body into overdrive. "Hi," she said in a voice that sounded too controlled even to her ears. "I see the ladies are still following you?"

"Hey." He took a seat across from her, removing his cowboy hat and placing it on the chair next to him. "Not as many as there have been, so I'd say our arrangement is working. Have a good day?"

She pretended not to notice the way his arm bulged when he carved a hand through his hair. She failed miserably. Godness, he was *hot*. "Quiet day," she told him. "I spent most of it at the coffee shop researching you."

He lifted an eyebrow. "Find out anything interesting?"

"Not really."

"Good. I'd much rather you hear about me from the source."

You and me both. She smiled instead of saying that aloud and was glad for the interruption when the waitress arrived at their table. Once she took their orders, she returned quickly with Colter's beer in a tall, frosty glass and Adeline's glass of pinot grigio.

"All right," Adeline said after taking a long sip of her wine. She savored the dry, crisp taste before taking her journal from her purse. "About that interview—"

"Nah, not just yet."

She blinked. "Not just yet?"

"We've got time to interview me later," he said, returning his glass to the table. "Tell me about you."

"Why?" she asked, baffled.

"I'd like to know about the girl who left Devil's Bluffs—" his heated gaze roamed over her "—and the *woman* who came back."

She shifted against her chair, wishing the restaurant had turned the air-conditioning on higher, but at his dancing eyes, she straightened. Women must drop to their knees for this man, and it was embarrassing how all that charm and killer smile made her want to do the same. "It's really not that interesting. We moved to New York City when my mom decided she'd had enough of small-town living."

"Your dad didn't care that you left?"

She swallowed the sudden emotion clenching her throat with another long sip of wine before answering him. "I've never met my dad."

"Ever?"

She shook her head. "After I was born, he didn't want to be involved, and my mother respected his choice."

"Brave woman."

"No one is better than my mother," she agreed. "She was everything I needed, so having an absent father wasn't really a big deal." At least that's what she'd keep telling herself until she believed it. "I think my mom only told me about him because I eventually asked."

"You don't want to meet him?"

"Not particularly," she answered honestly.

Obviously sensing she had nothing more to say on the matter, he shifted the subject. "You like it in the big city?" he asked.

"I love New York City," she said, playing with the

stem of her wineglass and noticing her fingers drew his attention. "I can't imagine living anywhere else on the planet."

His eyes lifted and head cocked. "It's not too loud?"

"Oh, it's loud, and a little bit smelly, too." She laughed. "It took a very long time to get used to being in a city. Devil's Bluffs has, what…ten thousand people?"

He nodded. "About that."

"So, yeah, it took a bit to settle into a city with so many people, but not only did I get used to it, it's weird now when things are too quiet."

"Must be an adjustment being back here, then."

She stared into the face of the guy who'd starred in all her teenage fantasies. "It sure is something."

His slow-building smile stirred her nerve endings. Keeping that heated stare on her, he took another long draft of his beer before asking, "Why is the promotion so important to you?"

The questions were moving closer to what she didn't want to talk about, but she couldn't withhold the truth. One thing she'd learned about interviewing anyone over the years was to stay honest about her life. How could she expect the same from anyone if she didn't reciprocate? But, oddly, what was normally uncomfortable to admit wasn't with Colter.

"It's important because my job is legit all I have left in my life." His eyebrows began to squish together, but she pushed on. "A week ago, I found out that my fiancé, who I'd been with for five years, Brock, was cheating on me with his secretary. Yes, it devastated me. Yes, I'm still heartbroken. And yes, I have no idea what I'm going to do when I get back home."

"Understandable," he said gently.

"But what I do know is that all my dreams, all my plans, were gone in a blink of an eye. So, now all I have left is my job, and instead of crying on the floor like the pile of dirty clothes that I feel like, I'm fighting for a promotion to make sure that when I go home I have at least one thing that I can look into the mirror at myself and feel proud about."

His face locked down tight halfway through her speech, his expression revealing nothing. Until he said, "Do you have a cell phone?"

"Yes. Why?"

"Grab it and come here."

She hesitated, watching him closely for any hint of what he was up to and repeated, "Why?"

A low chuckle escaped him as he waved her forward. "Just come here, will you? I won't bite."

She cursed her thoughts when she wondered, *But what if I ask you to?* She hesitantly reached for her cell in her purse and rose, sidling next to him. He had her on his lap a second later, and sitting on his lap felt good... *really good...too good...devastatingly good.*

"Unlock your phone," he murmured into her ear. "Take a photo of us."

She laughed nervously. "For real?"

"Indulge me," he said.

Her skin felt alive with sensation as she did as he asked.

When she set her camera to selfie mode and lifted the phone, his heated gaze engulfed her. Though it was her own eyes—and the raging lust in them—that stunned her more. She'd done love with Brock. He'd taken her virginity, and their sex life had been good. Lust, however—she'd never tasted this rich, needy desire that Colter evoked in her.

He licked his lips before brushing his mouth across her ear. She shivered, shutting her eyes against the yearning filling her, as he murmured, "Take the picture, Adeline."

She managed to reopen her eyes, finding his intense stare locked onto hers as she snapped the picture.

He leaned away, grinning. "Yeah, New York, post *that* on Instagram."

None of this is real. She repeated the words again and again in her head, reminding herself this was all for show, as she returned to her seat on shaky legs. Back in her chair, she didn't even recognize herself in the photograph. Her pupils were so dilated, nearly all the honey color of the irises was gone. Her cheeks were flushed deep red, and her lips were parted, begging for his kiss. "You do realize the mess this will create for me," she told him.

He grinned salaciously. "Trust me, if anything is going to piss off that prick who hurt you, it's going to be that picture."

The huge, gaping hole in her heart wanted Brock to hurt. Badly. Not thinking too much on it, she posted the picture, along with the caption "Nothin' beats dinner with a cowboy!"

When she set her cell down next to the silverware,

Colter raised an eyebrow. "Must feel good to show him what he's missing, right?"

"It does," she admitted, "but it feels better to feel like I'm something worth missing." Until the words left her mouth, she hadn't realized how Brock's cheating had made her feel. Worthless. She didn't feel worthless tonight with Colter.

"He's a fool if he's not missing you, Adeline." Colter's eye contact firmed as he leaned forward, closing the distance.

Rational—she'd always been proud of having that trait. Logical—she never swayed from doing the right thing. But her body wasn't screaming levelheadedness at her as she squeezed her legs together, desperate for friction against the ache between her thighs, yearning for his touch.

"The porterhouse?"

She jerked back at the waitress's squeaky voice, broken from the wild spell he'd woven around her. A spell leaving her drenched, trembling, breathing heavily.

"That'd be me," said Colter, his voice husky.

Blushing, Adeline kept her focus on the squash risotto placed on the table in front of her.

"Do you need anything else?" the waitress asked.

Colter gave a low, throaty chuckle. "A couple of cold glasses of water, please."

Adeline caught his devilish grin and laughed softly. "Yes, *ice*-cold, please."

When they left the restaurant and began walking along the lit-up Promenade, Colter's stomach was stuffed full, warm and satisfied. Truth was, he felt more comfortable than he had in a long time. So comfortable that when Adeline twined her fingers with his, he didn't even flinch. One look at the women sitting on the bench and watching them approach with hungry eyes indicated why she'd made the move. But he'd begun to enjoy the woman herself, beyond this deal they'd made. She shared her life's ups and downs easily, no matter how painful it was. He didn't possess that skill. And yet, *and yet*—he wanted her to know him.

Every word she'd said during dinner surprised him. She was funny, cute and fascinating—nothing like he remembered the awkward, shy kid who'd barely acknowledged the world around her. He gave her a quick look, finding her focused on the women they passed, wondering if her situation made her more appealing. She was leaving in two weeks. She'd *just* broken off her engagement. If there was any woman safe enough for him to enjoy some skin-to-skin pleasures with, Adeline was a safe bet. By the way she was squirming in her seat tonight, he'd also bet she was feeling the same way about him.

Her sweet laugh suddenly drew him out of his thoughts. "I have never had so many women give me dirty looks in my life," she said.

"I find that hard to believe," he admitted. He could barely keep his eyes off her and his thoughts PG-rated.

"Why is that so hard to believe?"

He took his time roaming over her face and didn't deprive himself of a glimpse at her spectacular cleavage. "You're beautiful, Adeline. Women get envious of that."

She blushed, quickly looking back ahead of her, paying attention to where she was walking. "It wasn't... I wasn't always like this, as you know. I was a late bloomer, and honestly, without my best friend, Nora, I'm sure I'd still be in a pair of overalls, lost in my journals."

An image of her, naked but for a pair of overalls, flashed in his mind, making his cock twitch. "You won't hear me object to overalls." He'd bet she'd fill them out in all the right places. "They can be sexy when worn right."

Adeline released his hand to nudge her elbow into him. "Nora would gut you if she heard you say that. She takes pride in the fact that she helped me find my sense of style."

"She's a good friend to you?"

"The very best of friends," she replied. "My life is better because she's in it. We're very, *very* close. Are you and Beau still like that?"

"We are," he said. "But I also have Riggs, the bartender at the Black Horse. He's my closest and oldest friend."

"Nice. I thought I recognized him last night. He went to the same high school as us?"

"He did, but he enlisted in the military after high school and then became a cop. He only opened the bar this last year."

Ahead, a German shepherd walking with its owner began barking at the border collie across the street. She waited until they passed and the dogs quieted before she said, "Okay, enough about me and my life. You promised me a story."

"You're right, I did." He gestured to the cobblestone pathway, hugged by big, mature trees, that headed into the park. "Ask away."

"From what I've learned, you lived in Seattle for a time. Is that true?"

He nodded, shoving his hands into the pockets of his jeans. "After I got married to Julia, we moved to Seattle. Did you ever meet her?"

Adeline snorted a laugh, pointing to herself. "Pigtails and overalls, remember? We weren't exactly hanging in the same circle of friends."

"Right." He paused, and then after thinking about it, he added, "You probably wouldn't recognize her now, anyway." Adeline watched him closely, and he knew he was revealing too much, but it felt wrong to withhold parts of himself, no matter the risk there. "Off the record?"

She inclined her head. "You've got my word."

He waited until they passed a couple picnicking in the gazebo before he began. "After we got married, Julia was hired by a big event-planning company out in Seattle. I had obtained my helicopter pilot's license for the ranch to oversee our cattle and land, but when we moved to Seattle, I was hired on by a company in the private sector that provides private helicopter and plane flights."

"I saw the award you got."

He smiled remembering that day and the pride he'd felt for a job well done. "I enjoyed my job there. I worked mainly with politicians and celebrities."

"Neat," she said. "You were happy out there?"

He shook his head. "I hated the big city, but we never planned on staying. The plan had always been for Julia to get a few years of experience, and then we'd come home."

"What were your goals?"

"Either to continue flying for a private company back here in Devil's Bluffs or work for medevac."

"You didn't want to open your own company?"

"I wanted to fly, not run a business."

"All right," she said after a moment of processing. "So, then, what changed?"

"Julia changed," he admitted, his cowboy boots clicking against the stones on the pathway. "The country girl I fell in love with vanished, replaced by a woman focused on high society and living a lavish lifestyle. She turned into a woman I didn't even recognize. A woman I had nothing in common with."

Adeline nodded in understanding. "Is that why you're not together anymore?"

"That's part of the reason." He gestured to a bench beneath a big shade tree and waited for Adeline to take a seat before he joined her. "It wasn't a single reason that ended the marriage. It was the accumulation of a few things."

"Do you mind sharing them?"

He probably shouldn't have, but, lost in the comfort of her kind eyes, he couldn't stop himself. "I want kids. She did, too, until suddenly that wasn't something she cared about. It was the bigger celebrity she met, the more expensive party, the dress that no one else had. And then, one day, she told me that she no longer wanted to have children."

"That ended it, then?"

Colter looked past the trees back to the road, trans-fixed by the twinkling lights glistening against the street. "I received a call one night from my mother, telling me that my father's Parkinson's had taken a turn for the worse and she couldn't look after him anymore." When he met Adeline's tender gaze, he liked how she listened, intent and tuned-in. "She begged me to come home. My father couldn't run the ranch anymore, and she needed me." A sour taste filled his mouth as he said, "When I asked Julia to come home, she said she wanted to stay in the city. Before I left for home, she asked for a divorce."

"Ouch, that's hard," Adeline said, her hand on her heart.

A nod. "That information I would prefer to keep out of the article, but what you can put in it is that I came home after my divorce and stepped into my father's role as CEO of Devil's Bluffs Ranch."

Adeline pulled her cell phone from her purse. "Sorry, is it all right if I take notes?"

"It's fine." He leaned back, placing an arm behind her on the bench, fighting against wanting to drag his finger over her soft shoulder.

"It must be hard for your dad not to be working. I always remember him being such a hard worker."

"I imagine all of what he's going through is hard," Colter admitted.

She agreed with a nod and made a few notes on her phone. "Are you happy to be back home, stepping into his big boots?"

"Yes."

Their gazes held for a beat. Of course, she called him out. "Liar," she said.

"That obvious, huh?" he asked with a snort.

"Yeah, pretty much."

He slowly drew in a big, deep breath before blowing it out his mouth. "It's not that I'm not happy to be heading up the ranch and taking over my father's role. I'm proud to be leading the Ward legacy, but it's that for the last handful of years, nothing in my life has been picked by me. My hand has always been played for me, and I don't like that." By the tenderness sweeping across her face, he knew he'd said too much. "Of course, that's off the record."

She gave a gentle smile. "How about we just say the emotional stuff stays off the record, so you don't have to keep saying that. All right?"

"Deal."

She hesitated as an elderly couple walked by, hand in hand, strolling into the still evening as the sun began to set, before glancing his way again. "When it comes to stepping into your father's role and becoming CEO of Devil's Bluffs Ranch, what do you want people to know?"

"That I'll take care of the land, give back to the community and honor the hard work my father has done."

She hesitated, her eyes searching his. "You know, if you ask me, Julia made a huge mistake letting you go."

He parted his lips to respond but found his voice gone. His body was screaming *yes*. His mind was screaming, *Don't repeat your mistakes. She's a big-city girl, and you already failed at love once with someone who'd prefer skyscrapers to cowboy boots.*

But the breeze carried floral scents as something passed

in the air between them. Something real and raw, and so foreign that he wanted to wrap himself around the wonderful feeling—when her phone slipped from her hands.

"Oops." She laughed nervously.

"I got it." He went down on one knee and reached for her phone.

When he offered it to her, their fingers brushed. That sudden touch simply became a tease. His mind wasn't leading him as he lifted his hand and stroked her cheek—it was only a response to how she looked at him. Gentle, and yearning for his touch, she was the most beautiful thing he'd ever seen.

Just like that, his body won over his mind.

Even though he knew she was a city slicker who hated his town and who was leaving after she had her story, he leaned into her. Her lips parted, a soft breath escaping, in the moment before his lips pressed to hers. She melted into his kiss, rising to the demand when she parted her mouth to let his tongue slip inside.

He kissed her. For a good long while. Until he broke away when he heard the chattering women behind him, gasping and giggling. He found Adeline smiling.

"You always kiss that good or is it because you're being watched?" she asked.

She thought he'd kissed her because of their audience, but she was dead wrong. He chuckled, brushing his thumb against her bottom lip, puffy from his kiss. "Can't blame a guy for wanting to put on a good show." He rose, slipping her hand into his. "Come on, I'll walk you back to the inn." Before he did something he did not want others watching.

Four

The next morning, Adeline woke up in the too-soft queen-size bed at the inn, surrounded by a wall of pillows. The morning sun gleamed through the window, revealing a room far too French country for her tastes. From the toile wallpaper to the frilly curtains and the floral patchwork quilt, everything about this space felt too...*happy*.

Suddenly reminded what she'd posted last night, and only now realizing that her boss might not approve of her getting so close to the subject of her story, she immediately checked Instagram. The photograph of her and Colter had earned a few hundred likes. Not enough for her editor to notice. Even this morning she could still see the heat brimming between them.

She hoped Brock saw the picture and choked on it.

With a sudden burst of happiness, she closed Instagram, realizing she'd missed ten calls this morning. Two from Nora. The rest from her mother. And a dozen more text messages urging Adeline to call them immediately.

She leaped out of bed, calling home first. Her mom, Lorraine, answered on the first ring. "What's wrong?" Adeline exclaimed.

"Adeline Marie, do you have anything that you want to tell me?"

Adeline spun, heading for the window to look outside, wondering if the world had blown up. When a quiet street greeted her, she sighed inwardly. She was proud her mother had gone back to school after they moved to New York City to become a therapist, but sometimes—like *now*—her knowledge as a therapist got mixed with a mother's intuition, and the invasion into Adeline's life was a bit much to stomach. "It's not what you think, and it's really complicated, but Colter was goading Brock with that photograph I posted on Instagram."

"What photograph on Instagram?" Mom paused. "I have not seen a photograph on Instagram. The photograph I'm talking about is the one of Colter proposing to you."

"What?" Adeline yelled before reeling in her voice. "Wait...*what*?"

"Go to Facebook, my dear. You've been tagged," Mom said dryly.

Adeline scooped up her laptop and jumped back onto the bed. She logged in and opened her Facebook account, finding thousands of notifications, but then she saw the post.

She recognized the woman's profile picture—she was one of the women from last night who'd been laughing with her friend after Colter had kissed Adeline. The woman's angle prevented her from seeing the cell phone Colter was handing her, and… "Oh my goodness, it looks like he is proposing to me."

"Yes, it certainly does," Mom agreed. "It's everywhere on your social media. All these strangers talking about you. Congratulating you, for heaven's sake."

Adeline blinked at her phone, wishing the room would swallow her up. "Okay, first, I'm not engaged to Colter."

"I should hope not."

"Second, it's not what it looks like. He was handing me my cell phone back. You just can't tell from the picture."

"Ah, I see," her mother mused. "That makes perfect sense, because don't you know that everyone kisses each other when handing over a cell phone?"

Adeline cringed. She nearly made up an excuse but knew she needed to do one better for her mother. "Okay, so I kissed him a couple times."

The silence on the other end of the phone was deafening. "Honey, be honest with me. Are you okay? If this is some rebound fling that you need, fine."

Adeline shuddered. "Mom, I know you're a therapist, but I don't want to talk about this with you."

Her mother ignored Adeline like she hadn't spoken and went on. "But if this is because of your broken heart and you are about to make a huge mistake that you will regret, come home."

Knowing that her mother would hop on a plane and

arrive in Devil's Bluffs if she thought Adeline was having a breakdown—and loving her for caring that much—Adeline said, "It's neither of those things, actually." She caught her mother up on her arrangement with Colter.

Lorraine paused for a long time once Adeline finished. "Kissing him is part of this arrangement?" she asked.

"It makes our fake relationship more believable to all the women who are hounding him," she said, but then she knew her mother would read right through her lie. "I might not be hating that part, though."

More silence followed, and Adeline held her breath as the long seconds ticked by. Until her mother's sweet, comforting voice filled the phone line. "Just remember, my love, that Devil's Bluffs is not an easy place for you to visit. Your emotions will be rocky there. Brock *just* broke your heart, and you are still reeling from that. Please keep your well-being your top priority."

Yeah, well, what if kissing a smokin'-hot cowboy is good for my well-being? Adeline gave her head a hard shake. *Not part of the agreement.* "I hear you loud and clear," she responded instead, "but honestly, I'm okay. I think coming here was good for me. It's like coming home, in a weird way. I think I needed to remember who I was before Brock, if that makes any sense."

"It does make perfect sense, and I support you," Mom said.

The one positive of having a therapist for a mother was no matter how much she got into Adeline's emotional status, she was encouraging all the way with her decisions. "Thank you. I love you."

"Love you, too, honey."

They said their goodbyes, with Adeline's promise to keep in touch.

Sudden footsteps sounded outside the door before they faded away. Sitting on the end of the bed and staring at her phone, fighting to understand how to deal with this shit show, she started when her cell began to ring.

Nora. She answered the FaceTime call and said, "I can explain everything."

Nora's eyes were bulging out of her head, her mouth open, no words escaping.

"It's not what it looks like," Adeline said.

Nora blinked.

Adeline sighed heavily, rubbing at the throbbing in her temple. "Last night, Colter and I went out for dinner..." She relayed everything that had happened. The good, the shocking, the sweetness and the sexiness, finishing with the moment when Colter got down onto one knee to give her the fallen cell phone. "I'm obviously not engaged."

Nora choked out a laugh. "Okay, good, because for a minute there, I thought you'd up and lost your mind."

Adeline plopped back against the pillows on the bed. "I can't believe this is happening."

"It's crazy how real it looks," Nora said, sitting behind her desk at work. "And hot—like, really, really *hot*. Especially the picture on Instagram."

"I know," Adeline breathed, still feeling the butterflies fluttering in her belly.

Nora's eyes searched Adeline's for a moment before she grinned. "Okay, so maybe all this isn't so bad?"

"Except it's turning my entire world upside down," Adeline pointed out. "How does this make me look? One week ago, I was engaged to Brock. Everyone at home knows he cheated." Because she'd emailed all their guests to explain the wedding was off. She hadn't sugarcoated that email. It probably wasn't her finest moment, but she'd figured simple wording—The wedding is off. Brock cheated on me—summed it up the best. "Even my mom is worried I'm hanging on by a thread."

"Who cares what anyone thinks?" Nora countered, waving her hand. "Just do you, girl, and do what makes you happy right now."

If only life was ever that simple.

A sudden hard knock sounded on her door. Suspecting the innkeeper was delivering her morning coffee, the way she had yesterday morning, Adeline jumped off the bed and whisked the door open. Colter's heated gaze roamed her from head to toe, reminding her she wore a nightie and nothing else.

"Nora, I have to go," she said.

"Is that a good idea?" Nora asked, her eyes dancing. "Next thing you know, you'll be pregnant."

Colter chuckled, looking out-of-this-world handsome in a light gray T-shirt and worn jeans, paired with a dark tan–colored Stetson.

Nora's eyes widened. "Oh, is that *him*?"

Adeline flipped the phone around. "Nora, meet Colter. Colter, meet Nora."

"Hi, Nora," Colter said with his charming smile.

"Okay, I see what all the fuss is about," Nora said, her voice chipper. "It's nice to meet you, too, Colter."

"All right, babe," Adeline said, turning the screen back to her.

Nora mouthed, *He is so friggin' hot.*

Adeline restrained her laughter, nodding in agreement. "I love you, but I need to go and deal with this."

"Good luck," Nora said. "Let me know if I need to get a maid of honor dress."

"That is not funny at all." Adeline groaned. She ended the call to Nora's rolling laughter.

Colter leaned in the doorway, filling up the space, arms crossed against his wide chest. "Hi, wifey."

"That isn't funny, either." With a huff, she tossed her cell onto the bed. She took out a pair of cutoff denim shorts, a bra, panties and a black shirt before slipping into the en suite and changing quickly.

When she came out and slipped into her black flats, Colter was sitting on the end of the bed. "Ah, come on," he said. "It's a little funny."

She snorted, hanging her nightgown on the hook on the back of the door. "I can't imagine any of this being funny to my ex-fiancé and his family, who are really lovely people even though their son is an asshole."

"I'm sorry about his family," Colter said. His mouth twitched. "But I'd pay cash to see that prick's face right now."

"Actually, so would I," she admitted, her broken heart squeezing in agreement. She pressed herself against the door, folding her arms. "So."

"So." He smiled, cool and collected.

Again, she huffed, tossing up her arms. "I have no idea how you can be so calm about all this. What a mess we made!" The ringing of her cell had her stepping toward the bed. One look at the screen, and her stomach sank. "Oh, God, please, no." She promptly answered her phone. "Claire, let me explain."

"You are brilliant, Adeline, just brilliant," her editor exclaimed. "You don't need to explain anything. You wouldn't believe the attention this is getting. Keep sending pictures draw this out for as long as you can. It's only going to push your article further."

Adeline gasped, "No, wait."

Oblivious to Adeline, Claire continued, "Keep it up, girl. Keep it up." The phone line went dead.

"Why. Is. This. Happening?" Adeline groaned, sliding to the ground, dropping her head into her hands. "My editor is thrilled. *Thrilled!*"

"Oh, come on," Colter drawled. "It's not that bad being engaged to me, is it?"

She peeked through her fingers. "Honestly, how are you handling this so well?"

He rose, his presence a wall of strength as he approached, offering his hand. "Because I have been in a bad situation. This isn't bad, so what is left to do but laugh about it?" She slid her hand into his, and he helped her to her feet. "For one, this only benefits me. Now I'm not maybe taken, I'm off the market. Two, once you go back to New York City, all this will die down. I'll tell everyone we broke up, and you can tell everyone that it was a big misunderstanding, and that's that."

She blew out a long breath. "I guess you're right. What is fretting about all this going to do?"

"See, I'm even making sense. Not too bad for a fiancé, right?"

She laughed, relishing the way the tension faded from her chest. "Definitely better than the one I had."

His fingers dragged against hers when he released her hand, and the move seemed deliberate. Her nipples puckered in response. "All right, New York, pack your things. Let's get you to your new home."

A cold wave hit her, any heat tingling in her limbs evaporating. "Pardon?"

One eyebrow slowly lifted. "You do plan on keeping your end of the bargain, don't you?"

"Ah, yeah, but where am I going?"

He leaned against the desk, folding his arms, giving her a knowing look. "No one in town will believe we're engaged if you're not living with me."

One second…

Another…

Then another…

"Oh, shit," she breathed.

Five

Twenty minutes later, Colter cursed when he drove up the laneway to his house. His mother and Beau were walking back to the truck parked at the porch steps. "The cavalry has arrived."

"Please tell me you have already talked to them," Adeline muttered. At his silence, she frowned. "Why aren't you saying anything?"

"Because, in this case, I think silence might work better to my advantage than saying the wrong thing."

She snorted a laugh.

Grinning at her, he parked his truck behind Beau's and turned off the ignition. By the time he was outside, walking around the hood, Adeline was already greeting his family.

"I never would have believed it if I hadn't seen it

with my own eyes," his mother said, opening her arms to Adeline. "Sweetheart, how are you?"

Adeline walked right into Beverly's arms. "I'm doing well," she said before stepping away from the woman who Colter knew for certain gave the best hugs. "Before you ask, no, I'm not engaged to your son. I'm really sorry about all this, Beverly."

"Don't be sorry, honey." His mother smiled fondly at Adeline. Colter remembered that his mother had always thought the world of Adeline and gave Beau trouble often whenever he gave Adeline any grief. "How about you just explain what's going on?"

Colter shoved his hands into his pockets and got a smirk from Beau before he turned his attention to Adeline as she filled his family in on the happenings as of late. He watched, impressed she didn't look to him for help once. Christ, he'd never seen a sexier woman in his life.

"So," said Adeline, wrapping up a story he never would have believed himself. "Is this all crazy? Yes. But it's actually working out for both of us."

Mom shook her head slowly, obviously taking the time to absorb all this insanity. "Well," she eventually said, "if you're not hurting anyone, and you're both getting something out of this, I guess that's good."

"The engagement part was not part of the plan," Colter explained to his mother. "I'm sorry if this causes you any trouble with your friends."

"It won't," she said with her warm, comforting smile. "I'll let the ones that matter know about the situation. The others who don't... Well, they don't matter."

"Thanks, Beverly," Adeline said. "I really appreciate it."

Mom took Adeline's hand. "Not a problem, honey. Whatever we can do to help you get your promotion, we'll do."

When Adeline finally acknowledged Beau, his brother gave Adeline a slow, inappropriate once-over. Colter shoved him on the arm, and Beau chortled, glancing back into her face. "Adeline." He took her into his arms, the hug lasting longer than necessary. "It's good to see you."

"It's good to see you, too," she said, stepping back. "You're much taller than the last time I saw you."

Beau grinned. "You're much more…"

This time, Colter punched him on the arm, and Beau burst out laughing.

Mom watched furtively before giving Adeline a knowing look. "As you can see, things haven't changed too much around here."

"That's a good thing." Adeline smiled, but then her smile fell. "Though I am so sorry to hear that Grant's been unwell."

"Thank you, honey," Mom said, her voice breaking. "It's been a hard journey for all of us."

Adeline reached out, placing a comforting hand on Mom's shoulder. "If it's all right, I'd love to come by and visit both of you while I'm here in town."

"Of course." Mom beamed. "Come by the house whenever you'd like."

"Wonderful," Adeline said, slowly dragging her hand away.

Beau cleared his throat, drawing all the attention, and

threw an arm around Colter's neck. "Well, since you two aren't engaged, congratulations aren't due." He grinned at Adeline. "Which means you can come by my place, too, anytime you want."

Colter elbowed him, and as Beau let out an *oof*, Colter growled, "Shouldn't you be getting back to work?"

"Beau, stop digging at them," Mom snapped in a stern voice.

Beau tipped his hat at Adeline. "Jokes aside, it is really good to see you. You're looking great."

She smiled. "Thanks. You, too."

Colter scowled at the back of his brother's head the entire time he headed for the truck. Before driving off, Beau threw him a grin. Ensuring his mother couldn't see, Colter gave him a rude gesture. His brother laughed as he drove off, a trail of dust following his truck down the laneway.

"You two really haven't changed, have you?"

Turning to Adeline, Colter said, "No, he's still as annoying as ever."

"Your relationship is cute," she said.

"Cute? Not sure I'd call it that," Colter countered. "He'll always be the annoying younger brother, but he's a good father to his son, Austin."

She stared after the truck heading off into the distance. "I wish my mom and I could've come for Beau's wife's funeral. It seemed so wrong to only send flowers, but I couldn't convince my mom to come back."

"Don't feel bad. I've got no doubt Beau appreciated knowing you were thinking of him." Leaving her at the porch, he returned to the truck, took out her bags from the back and then gestured her inside. "Come on, let's get you settled."

Once he unlocked the door, she followed him inside and he led her through the house to the right side, where the bedrooms were located. The master was on the left, and the two guest rooms were on the right. He entered the bigger of the two, which had an amazing view of the sunrise.

As she approached the queen-size bed with the cream-colored duvet and accent pillows that a designer had brought in after he built the place, Colter set her bags down. If the house had been his decorating style, it would have no style at all, but he had purchased the artwork on the walls at the gallery downtown to support local artists.

He stayed by the door, unable to take his eyes off her as she surveyed the room. He felt oddly comfortable having her there in his space. Damn, maybe he was lonelier than he thought. "You'll be okay here?" he asked, breaking the silence.

"More than okay." She turned to him with a smile that warmed something icy in his veins. "You've got a gorgeous home. When did you build it?"

"The year before Julia and I married." Leaning against the door frame, he folded his arms. "My dad's deal had always been that once Beau and I saved up enough for a down payment for a construction mortgage, we could pick a spot and build."

"So like your dad to always help you, but at the same time make you work hard to earn it."

Colter agreed with a nod. "Yeah, that's him pretty much summed up." He glanced around the room he rarely came into anymore. "I built this home thinking I'd start a family here." He'd imagined this space being a nursery. "Now, of course, it's a lot bigger than I need. But if I've learned anything from my divorce, it's to always expect the unexpected. Life rarely works out as planned."

"Truer words have never been spoken."

His smile felt more honest than it had in a long time. He jerked his chin toward the hallway. "Want a tour of the rest of the house?"

"Yes, please."

He showed her the other guest room, the large master bedroom, with the king bed and dark gray leather headboard and sleek black furniture, and where her bathroom was, and then he set out some towels for her.

When they ended up back in the open kitchen that overlooked the rustic dining room and living room, where a black leather couch rested in front of a big stone fireplace, with a flat-screen television in the corner, she said, "You know, this might actually be the best thing that could have happened."

He wasn't so sure of that. How was he going to stick to the rules and not make things intimate between them? His thoughts were indecent enough already without her sugary aroma constantly invading his senses. But they were in this *together*, apparently, and today was the first morning he'd gotten out of his truck downtown and a woman wasn't waiting there for him. The plan had worked. "Why is that?"

Her sassy grin pooled heat in his groin. "It's not often I get to live in the house of the person I'm writing about."

"Best be on my best behavior, then." Something he needed to constantly remind himself of with her around. He glanced at the clock above the gas stove. "I need to get to work, but I can call you later if you want to discuss meals for the week."

"Don't worry about that," she said, her eyes gleaming at the chef's kitchen. "I actually love cooking, so dinners will be mine."

"All right, that works," he said. "Since I suspect I'm up before you, I'll handle breakfast."

"What time do you wake up?"

"Five."

Her eyes widened. "In the morning?"

"Yeah, sometimes earlier."

She shuddered. "You're right, you're up first. Breakfast is yours. I'll head out later today to grab us some food. Just text me anything you need."

"Sounds good." He headed to a drawer and reached in, grabbing a set of keys. "Here's the spare set for the house and my truck. Use it like it's yours. Company pays for gas." He took out a fifty-dollar bill from his wallet and set it on the counter. "That's for my share of the meals. Maybe next week we can hit the grocery store together?"

"Sure, sounds like a plan."

He intended to leave her then and get his day started, but he hesitated and realized he owed her a story that included his day-to-day life now. "Got anything pressing to do right now?"

"Nothing urgent, just boring emails to get to. Why?"

"I missed doing my usual flight around the ranch

to check in on the cattle and horses. Before you get to those emails, want to—"

"Yes," she blurted out.

He chuckled at her all but bouncing as she followed him out the back door to the helicopter pad resting next to the hangar. He nearly purred at his sleek six-seater Airbus helicopter. Once he reached the chopper, he checked the weather to ensure clear skies before doing his preflight inspection. He finished, confirming the gas cap was secure, and then helped Adeline into her seat, assisting her with fastening her seat belt, pretending he wasn't enjoying every stroke of his fingers against her.

After securing her, he offered her the aviation headset. "Last part, so we can talk."

She settled it onto her head and beamed. "Ready!"

Again, he chuckled, not sure if he'd ever seen anyone so excited to fly with him. He finished his final walk-around inspection before getting into his seat, buckling up and sliding his headgear into place, adjusting the microphone over his mouth.

"Still ready?" he asked.

"Hell yes." Her voice sounded muffled through the headset, but her dancing eyes flooded his chest with warmth.

Focusing on his job—to keep them both safe—he confirmed the flight controls were in the correct position before he powered up the helicopter and lifted off, the ground moving farther away as the seconds drew on. Her loud squeal brushed across him, and he felt a rush of adrenaline storm through him.

"Okay, I can totally see why you love doing this," she said, staring out her window.

"I've always loved to fly," he admitted. "There's a freedom I find in it that I don't feel doing anything else. But the views also don't hurt. In Seattle, while busy, the skyline was quite beautiful."

"But not as beautiful as this," she breathed, awe in her voice. "I forgot how stunning it is out here."

He glanced out her window, finding the rolling hills of Ward land, grassy meadows as far as the eyes could see. The lake stretched along the west side, the cattle grazing next to it as expected. He circled them at a distance, not wanting to stir up trouble.

"What exactly are you looking for?" she asked.

"Calves, injured or sick heifers—anything that would need us to ride up to tend to them."

She glanced at him, sidelong. Damn near the sexiest thing he'd ever seen in that seat next to him. "If there was any of that, you'd send cowboys to this area?" she asked.

"Exactly," he agreed. "Smaller ranches would just ride out daily to check on their herd, but luckily for me, I have an excuse to fly out every morning when the weather cooperates." He gave the cattle one final look, not sensing or seeing any problems, before he turned east. "We'll check in on the horses now."

"Is Beau involved in that end of the company?"

He nodded, holding the yoke steady. "He was working toward becoming a champion reiner and riding for the USA team professionally when Annie passed away, so we hire riders now to show our horses for bragging and breeding rights."

"What does Beau do, then?"

"Handles all the sales and trains the horses before they begin to show. It's not quite what he dreamed of, but I know he enjoys his work."

She glanced out the front window, nibbling her lip before addressing him again. "And what about you? Do you enjoy your work?"

He smiled. "I get to do this every day. I feel fortunate for that."

She snorted a laugh. "You just avoided my question. You know that, right?"

"It's not avoidance, it's the truth," he admitted. Probably a little to himself, too. "I might not be doing what I love all the time, but my family needed me. Nothing comes before them."

"And that's why having all these women trying to hit on you was a distraction you didn't want?"

He nodded. "You got it, New York."

She watched him a moment and then gave him the sweetest smile he'd ever seen. "You know, you're making it very easy to write about you."

"Why is that?"

She glanced back out her window. "Because you're an incredibly good man."

Later that afternoon, when Adeline was sitting in a booth at the coffee shop, coins clinked into the tip jar at the counter from a paying customer as she recalled what she'd seen of Colter's house. When she began typing on her keyboard, the aromatic scent of espresso infused the air.

For all the money the Ward family is worth, the simplicity of Colter Ward stands out. The art decorating the walls of his house wasn't created by famous artists, but local artists who painted the beauty of Devil's Bluffs, a town he clearly loves.

"Is that the one?"

A sharp voice cut through the murmur of voices, past the radio playing in the background. Adeline took a long sip of her milky latte drizzled with caramel, tuned in to the women sitting at the table across from her.

An airy slurp of an empty cup. "Yeah, that's her. I don't see what's so special about her."

The old version of Adeline would have kept staring at her laptop, pretending she didn't hear them. But she wasn't that same shy teenager who was too afraid to speak up. She turned toward the catty women and cleared her throat. When they met her gaze, she said sharply, "What's special about me is that I'm really—like out of this world—incredible in bed." She might have laughed at their bulging eyes if she wasn't annoyed on both her own and Colter's behalf.

Staring them down, she could only smile as both women rose and quickly left the coffee shop. She began to understand why Colter had been desperate enough to make the arrangement with her in the first place. She'd never had so many women glare at her in her life and make snide comments. These women chasing him were like sharks.

With a sigh, she looked out the giant glass window with a view of the street, watching as cars and trucks drove by. She was returning her thoughts to her article when her cell phone dinged.

A quick look at the screen, and her mood soured further.

Brock had texted, Adeline, please, please call me.

She heaved another long sigh. For over a week, she'd ignored him, and that had been working, but she didn't reach her phone and dial his number for Brock's sake. She called for his parents, who had likely seen the photo, too, and whom she had grown close to over the years she and Brock dated. Deep down, she knew the breakup of their relationship wouldn't only tear apart her and Brock's lives, but it would affect those who loved Brock and had to look him in the eye after the terrible thing he'd done.

Brock answered on the first ring. "Adeline?"

"Hi, Brock," she said, leaning back against the leather booth.

"Thank you for calling," he breathed.

Hearing his tight voice was adding salt to an open wound, and it burned, reminding her she was still hurting. Deeply. "I take it you saw the article."

"I did. Is it true?"

A dry laugh escaped her. "No, of course not. It was a misunderstanding."

"That kiss didn't look like a misunderstanding."

She ground her teeth. "My life is not your business anymore." Her gaze fell to the barista behind the long counter stacked with chrome espresso and frothing machines. "I called so you could let your parents know what's going on. I'm sure this is all very confusing for them."

A pause, the thick whir of the frothing machine filling the silence. "They miss you," he said eventually.

She shut her eyes and breathed past the squeezing of her throat. "I miss them, too. Please let your mom know that I do plan on reaching out and I'll call her when I'm back in New York City."

A beat.

Then his voice blistered, "Adeline, please let's talk about this. I hate that everything happened like it did. I hate that I hurt you."

"I didn't call to talk about this," she snapped before reminding herself the conversation was pointless. But she hated the part of her heart that wanted so desperately to say *let's fix this somehow*. The part that still loved him, that believed they'd stay together forever, regardless of how he'd hurt her. "Please tell your mother what I said." She ended the call before he could say anything else.

Knowing she'd never get anything else done, she packed up her laptop and did what she always did when feeling down—she hit the grocery store. She bought all the ingredients for homemade cookies and spaghetti and meatballs, avoiding making eye contact with the women glaring her way for taking the gorgeous Colter Ward off the market.

Once back behind the wheel of Colter's massive truck, she ducked her head, hoping no one recognized her while she attempted to maneuver out of the parking spot. In New York City, she depended on public transportation, walking and the odd Lyft. She hadn't driven a vehicle in a long time—certainly not a truck that took up the entire road.

When she arrived back at Colter's, she found the house empty. Perfect. Standing in Colter's kitchen, she opened her Spotify account and played her pop songs playlist. As Lady Gaga's voice filled the kitchen, she shut out the world, her bleeding heart and all the confusion, and she did what always made her feel better—she began cooking.

It wasn't until the meatballs were simmering in the spaghetti sauce on the stove and someone cleared their throat that she realized she wasn't alone anymore.

She turned around on a gasp, holding the spoon in her hand like a knife that would never protect her.

Colter leaned a shoulder against the wooden beam separating the kitchen and living room, crossing his arms over his strong chest. "Sorry to interrupt your dance party."

She blushed all the way up to her eyeballs, hurrying to turn the Michael Jackson song down. "How much did you see?"

"All of it," he said, grinning devilishly. "Liked it, too."

She blushed for an entirely different reason now, suddenly becoming aware of the dirt smudging his face and hands, the outdoorsy scent clinging to him. And that they were very much *alone*.

"What's all this for?" he asked, gesturing to the snickerdoodle cookies cooling on the counter. Plus, the dirty pots and pans in the sink for the spaghetti dinner.

"I talked to Brock today," she explained, cringing at the mess she'd left. "When I'm upset, I cook."

He studied her. Then he smiled. "Let me take a quick shower, then I'll help you clean up."

Him. In. The. Shower. "Okay, yeah, sounds great. Spaghetti will be ready in a half an hour."

"Excellent."

While he headed off down the hallway, instead of imagining what Colter looked like soaking wet, with water beads trailing down his six-pack, she began cleaning up the mess.

By the time he returned from his shower, wearing gray jogging pants—that should be illegal for hot men to wear for the way they accentuated every masculine thing about him—and a black T-shirt with the ranch's logo on the front, she had washed up most of the messy kitchen.

Though he still grabbed the drying cloth and sidled next to her, beginning to dry and put away the dishes. "Heard you had some driving issues today," he said with a smirk.

"You did not," she gasped, splashing water into the sink.

He nodded, chuckling. "I got some complaints today about a slow driver holding up traffic."

"For real?" she countered, aghast. "Do people have nothing better to do than call you and complain?"

His mouth twitched. "I assume they thought you worked for me."

"Still, driving slowly isn't a terrible thing."

"Except for the people needing to get somewhere on time."

She flicked water at him, and he laughed easily, in a way that she never would have dreamed she could've made him laugh. Which got her thinking… "Can I ask you a personal question?"

He took a pan from the sink and began drying it. "Sure."

"You divorced a year ago. You're unattached, free to do whatever you want, so why, when I saw you in the bar that first night, were you so against the idea of a woman's attention? Most men in your situation would take full advantage of ladies chasing after them."

"Most men haven't stepped into a multimillion-dollar ranch they need to head up."

She scrubbed at a crusty spot on the saucepan. "So, you're not looking to date because you're too busy?"

He hesitated, giving her a long look. "Is the journalist asking me or the woman?"

"The woman," she said immediately. Before she realized she was edging the line of breaking their fake relationship's rules.

Regardless, he answered, "I'm not against the idea of dating again. I still want to grow old with someone and look back on my life knowing I did things right. Family has always mattered to me, and that hasn't changed."

"I sense a *but* in there."

Another hesitation. This time, the silence dragged on until he finally bowed his head to the pan he was drying. "But I'm not good at love."

Hoping he saw she understood, she agreed, "I'm not very good at it, either."

"I'm not so sure about that," he countered, opening a big drawer and placing the pan inside. "In your case, it seems you were blindsided by an insecure asshole who mishandled your heart."

"Yeah, well, I could say that in your case, it seems that you gave all of your heart to someone, and even that was not enough."

He snorted a laugh, flipping the towel onto his shoulder. "I suppose you could say that, but I'm sure I have fault in there somewhere, too."

She returned the smile. "And I'm sure I'm at some fault in my situation, too."

He leaned a hip against the counter, folding his arms. "How could you possibly be at fault for someone cheating on you?"

"I still haven't figured that out," she admitted, "but honestly, I haven't really figured out anything. I just packed for this trip and left all of that stuff back home."

She handed him the saucepan, and as he began drying it, he asked, "Did you suspect Brock was cheating?"

"No, and I think that was the hardest part. I had no idea anything was wrong. I'd been planning our wedding, so blind to everything."

"How did you find out?"

"His secretary, the woman he was cheating with, called me." It had been the hardest phone call she'd ever received in her life. Her soul had left her body that day, and only now was it beginning to feel like it was coming back. "I guess he'd been telling her that he was leaving me, but then she saw the wedding invitation and realized he'd been lying to her, too."

"He lost both of you, then?"

"Seems like it," she said with a nod. "Today on the phone, he was all apologies and wanting forgiveness, but he's probably saying the same thing to her. And you can't fix cheating."

"Once trust is gone, it's gone," he agreed.

"Yeah." She reached for the cookie sheet and began scrubbing at the burned cookie spots. "Did you suspect anything was going wrong with Julia?"

"Yes and no," he said, drying a big wooden spoon. "I knew she'd changed. She became more about fancy things than quality time. It was like the wealth in Seattle swallowed her up and she couldn't see a small-town life anymore. The woman I married changed until I didn't even recognize her anymore."

"So, what didn't you expect, then?"

A pause. "We had a miscarriage, and what I hadn't expected was her reaction to it."

"I'm really sorry for your loss. That must have been hard."

"It was," he said, "but to be honest, what I won't ever forget was the look on her face when we had the ultrasound, and it was confirmed we lost the baby."

"What did she look like?"

"She was relieved."

Adeline's hands stilled on the pan. "There's something seriously wrong with her if that was her reaction."

He gave a slight shrug. "Or she felt trapped and suddenly she realized she had an out."

Her heart reached for his as her soapy fingers touched his arm, fully aware of the flexing bicep beneath her fingers. "I'm so sorry, Colter. I can't even begin to imagine how difficult all of that must have been for you."

"It was the worst time in my life," he said gently. "But life does go on. I moved back here. She moved on with her life in Seattle."

"You haven't heard from her since?"

He shook his head. "Truthfully, I doubt we'd have anything to say to each other. We are two different people now."

"Was it hard coming back here without her?"

"At first, yeah, but then my focus became about my family and the ranch, where it should have been all along."

She slowly released his arm, although she struggled against keeping her hand against his warm strength. "Does that mean you feel bad that you moved to Seattle?"

"Bad? No," he clarified. "I made a choice, and I live with that choice, but I know I let my family down when I moved away." He bowed his head, his voice rough. "I let my dad down not taking over the ranch then. And I can't help..."

"Can't help what?"

He glanced sidelong, emotion burning in his eyes. "I can't help but wonder, if I'd stayed and let my dad retire, if he'd be better off than he is now."

She grasped his forearm again, pleading for him to hear her. "You cannot blame yourself for his Parkinson's. That's not on you, and the Grant Ward I know would never have retired unless he was forced."

"Maybe." He watched her closely...intently. Until

heat, and nameless things, simmered in the air between them.

She quickly turned back to the sink, but not before
Colter captured her chin, bringing her attention back
to his emotion-packed gaze. "I'm sorry for you, too,
Adeline."

"Thank you," she breathed, narrowing her focus on
his slightly parted, totally kissable lips.

What had felt a little sad now felt red-hot and needy.
His eye contact firmed, erasing the room around her.
She became all too aware of the racing of her heartbeat.
But as the timer on the stove beeped, indicating dinner
was ready, she took a step back, distancing herself from
what her body craved.

Him. Naked. Now.

Not part of the fake relationship!

Blowing out a slow breath, she quickly moved to the
stove and turned off the dial but dared to take one quick
look over her shoulder at him. Hard in every place that
mattered, he gripped the counter tight and watched her
with hungry eyes.

"Come on," she said, keeping things firmly in the
"not intimate" category. "Get it while it's hot."

He tossed the towel back onto the counter and
grinned. "Is that an invitation?"

Her mouth dropped open as she blushed up to her
hairline.

His laugh filled the kitchen as he grabbed a plate and
began scooping up noodles.

But as she filled her plate, she couldn't help but wonder... *What if it was?*

Six

Six days later, Colter dipped the helicopter to the right, following the cattle stirring up dust below. On the ground, the Devil's Bluffs Ranch cowboys were running the cattle to another pasture to prevent overgrazing. He was their eyes from above. A calmness settled over him as the sun glistened high in the sky over the meadow. He took solace when they rotated the cattle's and horses' pastures. It gave him more time in the air.

Below, a calf suddenly bolted left, breaking free from the herd. Colter stayed on the black calf. He said into the mouthpiece linked to an earpiece in the ear of Shane, a longtime cowboy on the ranch, "Lost calf on your ten o'clock."

Shane spun his horse and galloped toward the calf, until he guided him back toward the heifer frantically searching for her baby.

Colter circled back, staying atop the herd, following the cattle as ten of the best cowboys Colter knew, along with four Texas heelers, moved the cattle from one lake to another, where the grass had grown high.

Long minutes went by on the cattle drive. Colter embraced every single one where he wasn't stuck in a stuffy office, enduring long meetings and going over fiscal reports. This part of his job he loved, along with when he got his hands dirty, dealing with the cattle. His past was full of wonderful memories of the summers he spent on the ground with the cowboys. Those easy days were long gone. He missed fixing fence boards and simpler times.

When they eventually made it to the new pasture, the cattle settling into their new spot next to the lake, Shane looked up at the helicopter, giving a thumbs-up. Colter returned the gesture, then turned the helicopter to the left, returning home to a stack of paperwork and a couple meetings later this afternoon. His heart felt like it was shrinking as he spotted his house off in the distance. Just then, his phone rang through the interface in his headset. He hit the answer button. "Colter."

His mother's sweet voice filled his ears. "Hello, my dear, it's your mother, wondering if you'd like to come for lunch."

Lunch always meant *we need to talk*, but he'd never turn down one of his mother's home-cooked meals. "I can get there within an hour."

"Lunch will be ready," she said.

He ended the call and returned to his house, where

he completed the postflight inspection, disappointed his flight was over. He missed the days when he flew for most of his day.

Within forty minutes, and after responding to several important emails, he was on the road. Another fifteen minutes later, he was arriving at his childhood home.

The old, two-story stone farmhouse rested next to the largest barn on Ward land, where sick cattle were tended and recovered. A bunkhouse was to the west of the barn for any cowboys who preferred to live on the property, but his father paid his cowboys well and most had families living off property. The cowboys who stayed were younger men and women who preferred the cheap rent and board, since Dad never gave a cowboy a free ride.

Colter parked near his mother's car and entered the house. The smell of spices overwhelmed him. There wasn't a day he'd come home when his mother wasn't cooking or baking something for her family. He left his boots at the door and his cowboy hat on the hook, and he found his mother in the kitchen they'd renovated a few years back to brighten up the small space. "Smells delicious." He met her at the stove, dropping a kiss on her cheek.

"Hi, my sweet boy." She wore a yellow dress he'd seen many times. "You just missed Adeline."

Like he'd done a thousand times before now, he took a seat at the big island in the kitchen and waited for his mother to bring in a hot meal. "She was here?"

"Oh, yes." Mom stirred the homemade soup on the stove. "She's been stopping in for the last few days."

"To talk about me?"

His mother glanced over her shoulder with a stern look, pointing her wooden spoon at him. "Colter James Ward, we did not raise you to think that highly of yourself."

"It's not arrogance, it's confusion," he corrected. "If she's not talking about the story she's writing on me, what's she doing here?"

"She's come by to help with your father," Mom said, warmth in her voice, returning to stirring the soup.

He leaned his arms against the quartz countertop. "That's kind of Adeline to help you."

"She's good stuff, that woman. Always has been."

He'd known Adeline was different the second he set eyes on her in the Black Horse, but he hadn't known then what made her stand out. Adeline had a heart of gold. And that sweetness was changing him—he could feel it down to his bones.

It didn't take much for him to know this fake relationship was beginning to feel all too real. He knew the dangers, knew he'd never move back to the big city, but he couldn't help feel what he felt around her.

In the days he'd spent with her, he'd laughed more than he had in the last year, and every moment with her made the weight of the responsibilities piled onto his shoulders lessen. He began to forget all the things he'd lost when he moved home.

"There is a reason I called you over here," Mom said, interrupting his thoughts. She scooped some soup into a bowl. When she set it in front of him, she continued, "I received a call today about Elenora Davis's charity dinner in Dallas that we always go to." The charity benefited the children's hospital. A cause Elenora, a dear friend of his mother's, had always believed in. "I...forgot..."

He reached for the spoon she offered. "You're going through a lot, Mom. Cut yourself a break if you can't keep everything straight in your schedule."

She gave him a smile, but the warmth never reached her eyes. "I know you hate these kinds of fancy events, but—"

"It's fine. I'll go in your place."

Mom leaned against the counter. Her stare was pained. "I know you are sacrificing a lot for your father and me. We want you to know that we see all your sacrifices and appreciate everything you are doing for your family and the ranch."

"I'm not sacrificing anything," he lied breezily.

Her brows shot up, her look becoming all-knowing. "I am your mother. Have you forgotten you cannot lie to me?"

A rough laugh escaped him. "I'll never forget. You won't let me."

"That's right, I won't," she said, turning back to the stove. She fixed herself a bowl and then joined Colter at the island. "Why don't you ask Adeline to go to the gala with you?"

"Not a bad idea," he said, scooping up the beef soup. "It'd be a good way for her to see all the charity work that we do as a family. It'd be nice to see that in her article."

At the thick silence, he glanced sidelong at his mother. She smirked. "Is that really why you'd invite her?"

Now it was Colter's turn to stick his spoon out at his mother. "Don't be nosy."

"I'm not nosy," she said, her eyes twinkling. "Just curious. You haven't really been seeing anyone, and you two seem to be getting cozy."

"Forced coziness, don't forget."

Mom dismissed him with a wave. "Just because two people are forced to stay together doesn't mean feelings can be forced."

Shaking his head, he scooped up another spoonful of soup. "See, just can't help yourself getting nosy."

"Of course I can't. I'm your mother," she said.

Pondering whether to talk to his mother or not, he ate a spoonful of his soup. And another. And another.

Until he realized he wanted his mom's advice.

"It's a sticky situation," he admitted, his spoon clanging against the bowl. "She broke off her engagement just two weeks ago."

"Oh?"

"Her fiancé cheated."

Mom's hand flew to her chest. "Poor thing. That's just terrible. Who would do that to her?"

"An idiot," Colter said.

"Indeed." Mom nodded. "But I do see what you're saying. Wrong time. Wrong place."

"Wrong *everything*," he offered. "She's leaving to go back to New York City in a little over a week. Even if there is something there—and I'm not saying there is—starting anything between us seems…pointless."

"Happiness, no matter how short an experience it is, is never pointless." Mom paused to place a comforting hand on his arm. "You were dealt a hard blow with Julia. It's been a year since I've seen you smile like you do with Adeline. Any time you smile like that, it can't be pointless."

He stared down at his soup, considering her words. Before he glanced at her. "Enjoy the experience is what you're saying."

"Exactly." She removed her hand to reach for her spoon again. "Life is made of a thousand experiences. Some experiences are short. Some may be longer. But in this big, messy thing we call life, always look for the happy moments, the good people, and cling to them with all your might."

He knew his mother spoke from experience of what she was currently going through with his father's declining health. While this year had been hard, she had more than forty years of happiness to look back on. In the comfort of the woman who loved him unconditionally, he opened his heart. "Trying again is…"

"Terrifying?" his mother offered.

A nod. "Maybe even more so when there are obvious obstacles in the way."

She smiled gently and patted his cheek. "My boy, there is something worse than having nothing. It's having everything you could ever want but being too afraid to chase after it."

He absorbed her words, then wrapped his arm around her. "You are one helluva smart woman."

"Yes, son, I know." She smiled, patting his arm.

* * *

Seated behind his desk at the newspaper early in the

afternoon, Waylon asked, "What can I do to convince you to come work for me?"

Adeline looked up from her laptop after adding another thousand words to her article. She always wrote long and refined her piece during edits. In this case, especially so, since the words came easily. The Ward family donated to the library and high school and supported the Devil's Bluffs community. What had started as a fluff piece about a hunky cowboy was becoming so much more. She knew why—she was seeing Colter differently. He was no longer a teenager crush but a *man*.

Realizing she had yet to answer and her old mentor's soft gaze was fixed on her, she admitted, "I do miss it here." She shifted against the rock-hard wooden chair. "I miss the simplicity of a small town. The quiet. And yes, I miss *you*."

He chuckled. "Good."

Where she sat at the desk next to him, the space was the same size as her editor's corner office in New York City. Newspaper articles were pinned on the four walls, along with historic pictures of Devil's Bluffs' past. "Every memory from my co-op here is a good one," she told him.

"See, if that isn't a good enough reason to move back, I don't know what is." Waylon winked. He took a sip from his mug that read, Of Course I'm Awesome. I'm an Editor. A gift that likely came from one of his two adult children.

Adeline envied how Waylon made his marriage work. How he loved his children. She wanted all those things. Now… She shook her head, not allowing herself to fall into a deep hole she would never crawl out of. "If only it was that easy to just snap your fingers and change your life," she said. "I miss writing the stories I did here."

A sparkle hit Waylon's eyes as he opened a drawer and took out a folder. "These ones, you mean?"

"You did not keep them," she said, quickly moving to his desk and accepting the file folder.

His smile shined. "Just have a look."

Moving back to her desk, she opened the folder, heat radiating through her chest. "Oh my goodness. I can't believe you kept them."

"Of course I did," Waylon countered. "You were so proud of all the stories you did. I didn't have the heart to throw them out."

She began fingering through the old articles. The very first time her writing ever made it into a publication. From the Christmas musical at the elementary school to the elderly-animal adoption at the animal shelter to the pumpkin-carving competition at the fall festival. She'd covered all the town's events, telling the stories of the people who passionately supported the community and brought people together. "This is amazing," she said, but then she stopped breathing when she reached one article.

Daddy & Daughter Dance Raises $20,000 for Kids' Cancer Foundation.

Adeline's eyelids suddenly felt gummy as she read over the words she'd written so long ago. Words she remembered were the hardest she'd ever wrote, drawing on something cold and hurting deep from her soul, reminding her, *Your dad did not want you.*

"I remember that article being difficult for you," Waylon said.

She started, not having realized he'd come to stand by her.

Swallowing back her emotions at the dreaded memory of having to attend the event without her father, she managed, "It was very hard."

Father's Day, bring your kid to work, sports games—all those times when a father was necessary had always been hard growing up, but none had been quite like the dance, when she'd been forced to watch happy daughters dance with their proud dads. "But it got easier, because luckily for me, I had a really great stand-in father to make that night one to remember."

"Still one of my favorite nights," Waylon said, squaring his shoulders. "Even got you out on the dance floor."

"Plus, you bought me the prettiest corsage."

"You were the prettiest girl there."

She felt breathless watching him. This man from her past who gave her so much without ever asking for anything in return. "You know, it's odd, but I thought coming back home was going to be so hard."

He leaned back against his desk, folding his arms over his faded button-up. "It hasn't been?"

She shook her head. "It's been the exact opposite. Maybe it's because what happened with Brock was so terrible." She'd caught Waylon up on her recent breakup this morning over coffee and warm croissants from the bakery. "So now anything else that happens doesn't seem as bad. But being back here has been like walking down a wonderful memory lane. I think I forgot how delightful everyone is here."

"Revisiting the past can be a good thing," Waylon agreed with a gentle smile. He returned to behind his desk. "Even the hard parts. Sometimes with a new perspective, everything can look different."

"I think that's very much true," she agreed, returning the smile.

Turning her attention back onto the folder, she began skimming through her articles when her cell phone beeped. One look at the screen, spotting Colter's text message, and her heart leaped up into her throat.

Got any plans tonight?

Gathering herself, she blew out a long breath and then texted back, Not that I know of. Why?

There's a charity gala in Dallas I need to attend on my parents' behalf. Interested in tagging along?

She gawked at the text and reread what he'd written a couple times over. Was this a real date or a fake one? It sounded like a real date. Should she be dating? This was too soon.

"Whatever you're overthinking, stop it," Waylon interrupted, not bothering to look up from his desk.

Adeline snorted, shaking her head at him. Most times she hated having such a readable face. Then she decided to take Waylon's advice, texting back, Sure. Besides, she was writing an article about Colter's life. Of course he'd want to show her these charity events.

Though the little voice in her head screamed at her, *This is a date*.

She finished texting, I'll need to grab a dress. What time are we leaving?

I'll fly us there. Leaving at 5. If you're up for it, I'll book us at the Rosewood Mansion for the night and we can fly home in the morning.

I'm up for it. Hell, suddenly she was feeling up to anything, everything and whatever came in between. And *that* was confusing.

She watched the three little dots, waiting for his text. His response came a few seconds later. Good. Tell the dress store to send the bill to the ranch.

She began responding that she'd feel terrible if he paid and she'd buy the dress herself, when his response popped up.

The ranch pays for my suits, too. Don't feel bad and obligated to buy the dress yourself.

Well, she did feel obligated. She'd always felt weird when men bought her anything. Her therapist had indicated it came from her never wanting to depend on a man, since her father had failed her, but she didn't want to make a big deal out of this, either. She began typing, Okay, then, I won't. Can I donate the dress after to someone needing a prom dress? She remembered the program from when she was in high school.

That's a great idea. We'll donate one of my suits, too.

Awesome. See you by the helicopter at 5.

Looking forward to it.

"Let me guess—you took my advice and that's what got you smiling?"

She laughed, catching Waylon's smirk. "Of course I took your amazing advice. That was Colter. He invited me to attend a charity event in Dallas tonight."

Waylon's brows rose. "Oh?"

"Don't look at me like that," she said sheepishly. "We're going as friends."

His brows rose higher. "In my experience, a woman only smiles like *that* when she's got something to smile about."

She tried to hide her blush, rising from her seat. "A reason to buy a new dress is always something to smile about." She gathered up her things. "Do you mind if I come back in a couple days and work here again? It's been nice."

"Adeline, you are always most welcome," he said. "You're even welcome to come back and take over when I retire."

She froze midway to shoving her cell phone in her purse. "You're retiring?"

He leaned back in his chair, watching her closely. "Well, it's about time. I'm pushing sixty-five."

It seemed impossible to even imagine the newspaper without Waylon. "What will you do then?"

"Marjorie wants to travel. We're talking about selling the house and downsizing. Then we'll set off to see some of the world."

"You deserve that," she said, and she meant it. "How absolutely wonderful for you and Marjorie. Do you have someone who is stepping in for you as editor?"

"Oh, I'll find someone suitable," he said, "but that's why I asked if you'd come back. I'd rather it be you that takes over my beloved newspaper."

She closed the distance and threw her arms around him, feeling like the world for this second seemed so full of love. "Your trust in me is appreciated, but New York City is my home now."

"Then I'm happy for you," he said softly.

When she leaned away, the reality of a cruel, cold world rushing back in, he flicked his hand, dismissing her. "Now go. Be wild and free. Make terrible decisions."

She slid her laptop bag's strap over her shoulder. "You never would have said that to me before."

"You're right, I wouldn't have told a sixteen-year-old girl that," he said with a sly grin. "But you're not that young girl anymore, are you?"

"No, I certainly am not."

Seven

Even after the forty-minute helicopter flight to Dallas, Colter still couldn't take his eyes off Adeline. Ever since she came out of the guest room and left him speechless. Dark makeup surrounded her eyes, making the honey color warmer. The sexiness of the long, slinky black dress she wore had him wiping his mouth. Her bright red–painted lips brought…*hunger.* A desperate ravenousness that was becoming harder to ignore.

Once they arrived at the Hotel Crescent Court in the art-centric part of Dallas, Adeline exited the Escalade the hired driver had picked them up in, and Colter's fingers twitched to reach for the back of her dress that was cut low and stroke the soft skin. Her hair was up, revealing the long line of her neck, tempting him to slide his tongue right *there*. But even as lust battered his senses, he knew more was going on between them than lust alone. And he wasn't sure what to make of that.

"Would you like me to bring your bags to the Rosewood Mansion, sir?" the driver asked Colter.

"Yes. Thank you," Colter said, shaking the driver's hand. "I'll reach out when we're done here."

"Excellent. Enjoy your evening."

As the driver returned to the Escalade, Colter narrowed his attention on the stunning woman gazing up at the trellises on the exterior of the grand hotel.

"Good heavens," Adeline gasped, "this place could rival any upscale hotel in New York City."

"It is stunning," he said, "but nowhere near as stunning as you in that dress."

"Thank you." She looked him over the way a lioness studies its prey before she pounces. "You're not looking too bad yourself, cowboy."

"I'm glad you approve," he said, heat flooding him.

How tempted he was to call the driver back and take them to the hotel instead. But, like a cold bucket of ice water pouring down on his shoulders, he remembered he had a role to play tonight. Best he play it.

"Before we go in," he told her, reaching inside his suit's inner pocket and offering her the ring he'd put there for safekeeping, "I thought it made sense for you to have this."

Her eyes widened before her brows lifted. "Are you sure this isn't a bit early in our relationship?"

He barked a laugh. "Probably, but life is better when you take some risks."

"Touché." She echoed his laughter and offered her

hand. "I guess it does make sense to have a ring if we're meant to be engaged."

"Mmm-hmm," he agreed. He slid the ring onto her slender finger. "This ring belonged to my grandmother. She would've gotten a real hoot out of this arrangement we've made. She had an amazing sense of humor."

"I wish I'd gotten to know her better," she said sweetly. "Gosh, her ring is gorgeous."

"A near-perfect fit, too." He had no doubt his grandmother would have gotten a hoot out of that, too. He offered his arm. "All right, the future Mrs. Ward, ready to go enjoy ourselves?"

She linked her arm with his. "You do know all of this is incredibly weird, right?"

"Weird, yes." He led her through the main doors of the hotel, walking past the doorman holding the door open. "But as far as I'm considered, weird doesn't feel all that bad."

A pause. Then her dazzling smile hit him straight in the chest. "You're right, it doesn't."

He passed people he recognized from other charity events. The rich and famous of Texas who all came together to support a cause.

"Colter," a banker Colter had met before called the moment they reached the hallway leading to the ballroom. "Wasn't expecting to see you tonight."

Colter shook the man's hand. "I would not have missed it." He turned to Adeline. "Let me introduce Adeline Harlow, a journalist out of New York City."

The man's eyes gleamed at Adeline. "Very nice to meet you, Ms. Harlow."

"You as well."

It took another ten introductions before they finally made it inside the ballroom. Vaulted ceilings topped high walls with crown molding and glossy hardwood floors. Waitstaff circulated the crowd to offer canapés and switch out empty champagne flutes for full ones. Colter arrowed for the bar, needing a hard drink more than ever. After greeting the white-gloved bartender, Adeline ordered a glass of wine, and he a scotch on the rocks.

After the bartender delivered their drinks, Adeline asked, "This isn't your type of thing, is it?"

"No," he said, placing a hand on her lower back, guiding her off to the side of the bar. "I've never been much of a schmoozer."

"Oh, I find that hard to believe," she said with a laugh. "You were all charm back in high school. I remember some of the teachers eating out of the palm of your hand."

"She's not wrong there."

Colter's muscles went rigid in a heartbeat. The soft music playing around them dulled in his ears. His focus narrowed on Adeline's gaze shifting over his shoulder. Her lips tightened.

Not particularly wanting to, but feeling obligated, he turned around and expected to see his ex-wife. Instead, he found a stranger. Everything about Julia had changed since the last time he'd seen her. Her blond hair was now a lighter shade. Somehow her eyebrows were darker and thicker. The lashes on her brown eyes were not hers. Her cheekbones, lips, face shape—even the large amount of cleavage popping out of her red dress—

did not belong to the woman he remembered. "Hello, Julia," he said cordially.

She smiled, though her face hardly moved. "Hello, Colter." Her cold eyes shifted to Adeline. "I'm sorry, you look so familiar. Do we know each other?"

"We do, actually," Adeline said. "Adeline Harlow. We went to high school together."

"Adeline," Julia said, mulling over the name. "Your face is familiar. I'm not sure I can place your name."

Colter nearly took Adeline's hand and drew her back, wanting to keep her far away from this part of his past, but Adeline said in an easy tone, "That's not very surprising. We didn't exactly run in the same circles."

"Ah, that must be it," Julia quipped. To Colter, she asked, "Where's your parents? I thought they always attended this event."

"My dad is not well enough to do these events anymore," Colter said.

Julia's hand pressed against her chest, her voice sounding sincere. "I'm so very sorry to hear that."

Colter inclined his head in thanks. "What brings you to the event?"

"Oh, my boyfriend is on the board of the children's charity," Julia said, bringing her hand to her diamond necklace, fingering the delicate band. "We arrived in Dallas a couple days ago but don't plan on staying long."

The murmur of many voices filled the air as Adeline said, "The hospital does such amazing things for little ones and their families. What an amazing charity to be a part of."

"Yes, it is," Julia agreed. "My Bronson gives so much of himself and his time to many charities."

Colter had never felt the urge to roll his eyes. Until now. Though when he caught the well-dressed dark-haired man approaching them, he figured a fight at a charity dinner was not how the night should go.

"Bronson, come," Julia called, waving her hand at him.

Colter knew the man. They'd met the tech billionaire through a friend Julia had made. "Bronson," Colter said when the man reached them, offering his hand as a sign of peace. "It's good to see you." Oddly enough, he felt no jealousy, no anger, *nothing* at the thought of this man being with Julia. Though he did wonder if Bronson knew the income Julia received wasn't from her failing company but came from Colter's own pocket.

"Nice to see you, too," Bronson said, returning the firm handshake. His dark eyes shifted to Adeline. "Bronson Bailey."

"Adeline Harlow," she said and shook Bronson's outreached hand before pressing herself against Colter, bringing a wallop of heat. Suddenly feeling a whole lot better, he wrapped his arm around her as her eyes twinkled. "I'm Colter's fiancée."

"Fiancée?" Julia repeated, giving Adeline a harder look now, reassessing, before she pulled back her surprise and put on a smile. "Oh, that's nice. I hadn't heard the news."

Colter locked his hold around the warm, spectacular woman in his arms, aware of the game Adeline played. "We haven't officially announced the news."

"We like our privacy," Adeline told Julia. She angled

her head, pressing her hand against his chest. "Don't we, babe?"

Damn if he didn't like her calling him *babe. Probably a little too much.* "Yeah, that's right, we do." Leaning down, he pressed his mouth to hers, momentarily wishing they were anywhere but there. And it wasn't until he felt her melt against him did he know for certain he was kissing her not for the show, but all for himself.

He'd broken the single rule of their fake relationship, and he didn't feel the least bit bad about it.

When he broke away, her dilated pupils greeted him. Rosy cheeked, she gave him a breathless smile when a bell began ringing, indicating everyone should take their seats for dinner. Acknowledging Julia and Bronson again, she said, "We should really get ourselves settled at our table. We hope you enjoy yourselves tonight."

"You as well," Bronson said.

Colter had begun leading Adeline away when Julia gasped, "Your grandmother's ring."

He spotted the ire in Julia's eyes, only now remembering that Julia had wanted the ring when he proposed. "It turned out my mother could let the ring go after all." At the reddening of Julia's face, Colter said to Bronson, "Enjoy your evening."

Guiding Adeline toward the circular dining tables covered in white linens and gold-edged china place settings, he wondered if the very reason his mother had given him the ring—which she'd said she could never part with—tonight was because she knew Julia had planned to attend.

He couldn't fight his smile.

* * *

Feeling slightly warm from the two glasses of wine she'd drunk during the salmon dinner, Adeline gladly followed Colter onto the dance floor. He settled them into an open space between dozens of dancing couples, the musical instruments harmonizing, as he spun her once before bringing her tight against him. She noted he'd lost his coat before dinner, rolling up his sleeves. Somehow, he looked even more handsome.

The slide of his hand low on her back, matched with the smell of his woodsy cologne, made her dizzy. She still couldn't quite believe how nicely he filled out his black-and-white suit with a thin tie. Add his black cowboy hat, and Colter had never suited the most-eligible-cowboy definition more.

The live band played Etta James's "At Last," and Colter easily guided her through the dance like he'd done this a thousand times before. "How, and when, did a small-town cowboy learn to dance this good?" she asked.

He dipped his chin, hitting her with warm eyes. "Julia made me take lessons before we got married."

"They most certainly paid off."

His smile was made of naughty things that made women's panties disappear. "I'm glad you think so."

My God, he felt good. Smelled so good. Heat spiraled through her in no way she'd ever experienced with any man. *Why don't I want to take this any further, again?*

Desperate to find any sense of her sane mind, she focused on the band, lost in the song they were playing, and she exhaled slowly. Talking. That had to cool the jets. "Seeing Julia must have thrown you off tonight," she asked, distracting herself from his hot, *hard* body.

"Actually—" he pulled her in closer, sprawling his hand just above her bottom "—it didn't throw me off at all."

She swallowed, suddenly aware of every spectacular line of him. "That must be unexpected."

"Unexpected, yes, but good," he agreed. "It lets me know I've healed what needed to be healed from that relationship."

"You should feel proud of that. I wish I could even begin the healing part."

His eyes searched hers, his hand pressing tighter, bringing her even closer, an odd sense of safety swelling. "It's been a year since Julia and I ended things. You can't compare our relationships."

"I guess you're right," she said, "but at least you can face Julia. I haven't done that yet. I've only talked to Brock once, and that was to make sure his parents were okay after the news of our fake engagement broke."

"You'll talk to him when you're ready," Colter said with a slight curve to his mouth. His thumb stroked slowly across her back. "Though I, for one, don't think you owe that man a damn thing or a second more of your time."

She instantly regretted the open-back dress for the access it gave him. "Thanks." Desperately trying to ignore the building heat seeping into her from his touch, she pressed on, "Why did seeing your grandmother's ring ruffle Julia's feathers so much?"

"After my grandmother passed away, Julia said she

wanted the ring. I asked my mother if I could have it when I planned to propose to Julia, but my mom said no."

"Why?"

He shrugged. "My grandparents were married seventy-two years. I think, for my mom, the ring is a symbol of our family. I'm sure it's hard to part with."

Adeline agreed with a nod. "I'm pretty sentimental about stuff like that, so I totally understand. But no wonder that dug at Julia a bit. I should have flashed it around more, like she was flashing around that necklace."

He chuckled. "Noticed that, too, did you?"

"Of course I noticed," Adeline said with a huff. "It's impossible not to notice how much she's changed. She doesn't even look like herself anymore."

"No, she doesn't," he agreed. Then his voice dipped lower, becoming throatier. "However, I'm not looking at her tonight." He pressed himself into her, leaving no space between them. "I'm looking at you."

Fake relationship. Fake relationship. Fake relationship.

Heat spiraled low in her belly, and soon, all she knew was his hefty erection pressed against her. The other couples dancing all faded away—even the music seemed to stop as he brought his mouth near. She asked in a rush, "If your mother had your grandmother's ring, how did you get it for tonight?"

"I asked her for it." His eyes searched hers before lingering on her mouth. "Perhaps it's not so hard giving something away when you know the engagement isn't real."

Yes, see, a fake relationship. "I imagine that's very much true."

His attention slowly lifted to her eyes again, and his

smile nearly melted her bones. "Are you truly interested in this or are you trying to distract yourself?"

She cursed the blush rushing to her face. *Get it under control, girl!* She considered what to tell him and what to keep private, but she decided she wanted him to know her, considering all that he'd shared with her. "The truth is, being here with you, dancing like this—" *feeling your massive erection* "—would make my teenage self die from happiness."

His brows drew together. "What do you mean?"

"I had a big crush on you all through school," she said quickly before she chickened out.

His thumb stopped its dance on her back. "Did you really?"

"Yes, big-time," she admitted with a laugh. "I was such a cliché. The girl staring at the guy from afar, daydreaming you'd come over and notice me."

"I had no idea," he said, his thumb resuming its slow dance along her skin.

"It's for the best, really. I had big daddy issues and I probably would've ended up in a bad place if any guy noticed me back then."

"You don't have those issues now?"

She shook her head. "Years of therapy helped with that, and growing up, too, realizing that life isn't perfect. People aren't perfect. And whatever happened with my father is on him, not me."

"That's a good realization."

She swayed her hips, following where he guided her. "It is, but it also doesn't stop me from wondering about him. Who he is now. What he's like."

"I think that's natural," he said. "But I also think he doesn't deserve you, either."

She couldn't fight her smile. "See, you are totally crushworthy."

His voice lowered, even deeper this time. "Does that mean you still have a crush on me?"

"Aren't all the girls crushing on Colter Ward right now?" she teased, and he chuckled.

Beneath her dress, her nipples puckered, an all-consuming need filling her with every slide of that thumb across her flesh. "But it's different now," she continued, "because back then you were the hot guy I couldn't stop looking at. You barely said a word to me. I made you into this perfect guy in my mind. But the thing is, you've grown into this incredible man. I think that actually makes you hotter."

He stopped dancing then. Intensity flashed across his expression. "I wish I saw you then like I see you now. I'm sorry I didn't."

Promises were in his eyes. Heated promises. Sweet promises.

Promises that at any other point in her life would have been the greatest thing to ever happen to her.

The room began to squeeze her as this fake relationship suddenly became all too real, the air becoming thin and impossible to inhale. Turning away, she booked it for the French doors with thick velvet drapes on either side.

Once outside on the balcony, she was surrounded by lush greenery and flowers of all colors, with gas-powered lanterns casting a warm glow into the night. She made it swiftly to the wrought iron railing and gulped at the air, feeling like her skin was on fire.

"Did I upset you?"

At Colter's low, regretful voice, she turned to face him, gripping the railing tight. "You didn't upset me." Holding his stare, she knew the moment he realized what was wrong by the way his expression became taut…*penetrating*.

He took a step toward her.

She held up her hand. "I need a minute."

"Do you?" he murmured. "Or do you need something else?"

A whimper escaped her, her knees weakening with every step he took.

Closer.

And closer.

Until he stood directly in front of her.

She fought to slow the racing of her heart, which was beating faster and faster. "What are we doing here, Colter?"

His hands came next to hers on the railing, the strength of his body encasing her. "Seems pretty self-explanatory to me."

Her head was screaming *no*. Her body was screaming, *Kiss me. Now!* "This is supposed to be a fake relationship, remember? We made rules that we are breaking. This is a terrible idea."

"Actually, I don't think it is." His lips met hers then, hot and wicked, and as his tongue slipped into her mouth, her hesitation evaporated.

She realized with his sizzling kiss that she was fooling herself. She'd wanted this to happen from the second she saw him again. And while her battered heart refused to jump into this game, she could do what Waylon had suggested: *Be wild and free. Make terrible decisions.*

Tonight!

When his hands braced her face as he angled her head, deepening the kiss, she felt her body rise to his challenge. The need flooding her to not think, to just… *indulge.*

"You have a past," he said, trailing scorching kisses down her neck. "I have a past. None of that matters now, don't you feel that?" He slid a hand down over her bottom, thrusting her against him. "Don't you feel this? *This* is all that matters now. I want you, Adeline." He nipped at her jawline before looking her in the eye again. "Do you want me, too?"

Safety. Comfort. Strength. Colter was all those things. But he was something more, something *tempting.* Something special that made her decision all too easy. "Yes, I want you." She grasped the front of his shirt, and before she met his challenging kiss with one of her own, she purred, "Preferably right now."

Eight

Colter kissed *her*. Roughly. Passionately. On the ballroom's balcony. Outside in front of the Hotel Crescent Court while they waited for the driver. In the back of the SUV on the drive to the Rosewood Mansion. In the elevator on the way up to their room. Urgency had nearly had him paying for a room near the ballroom, but he never stayed at the same place as an event—keeping business and personal separate always worked for him. But instead of taking her then and there, he hesitated for one important reason.

He didn't want Adeline to regret him.

So, he gave her time.

Time to change her mind.

The moment he shut the hotel room's door and turned back to the lavish room with king-size canopy bed and antique furnishings, he realized his worry was without reason. She stared at him hungrily, obviously feeling the same all-consuming need he couldn't ignore. Not anymore.

Breathless, he pressed his back against the door as she tucked a finger under the thin strap of her dress, slowly pulling it down. Until the fabric slid down along one bare breast. Colter's cock hardened to steel so swiftly he groaned as she revealed one taut, rosy nipple.

"Adeline," he murmured.

"You want to see more?" she rasped.

"Definitely more." He groaned.

Nibbling her lip, her cheeks flushed bright red, she repeated the move on the other strap of her dress. The fabric slowly slid down until her dress pooled at her feet.

Colter took in the view…*stunned* by what he saw as she toed the dress off to the side. Her curves were perfect. The gentle lines of her body were perfect. She was perfect. Bare on top, the only fabric she had on were black lace panties. He'd seen women naked. He'd even seen beautiful women painted in pictures. Movie stars on the big screen. No one came close to Adeline.

"You're so damn beautiful," he told her.

Her chest rose and fell with her heavy breaths when she reached up to remove her panties.

He tsked. "Those are mine to take off."

"Oh?" she asked playfully. "Then why don't you get over here and take them off?"

He locked the door behind him and then approached, allowing himself the time to look his fill at her. Her breath hitched when he reached her, taking her chin in his grip. "I might have been your crush, Adeline, but believe me, right now, you are mine." He saw the effect of his words, the way she softened. Her hands tangled into his shirt, and he helped her with the buttons.

Needing more of her, he sealed his mouth across hers as she brushed the fabric over his shoulders. When she reached for his pants, he let her unbuckle his belt, but he assisted her in shoving them down. He never stopped kissing her. Not when she explored each part of his body, like he was a prize she'd been waiting to claim. Not when she broke the kiss to look at his hardened length, discover the size of him. Not even when she gripped his cock and stroked him gently. He groaned and kissed her chin, her neck, her breasts, nipping at her nipples, unable to get enough of her.

Only when her hands slid back up his arms did he stop and drop to a knee in front of her. Her cheeks were flushed bright with color, her eyes wide as he tucked his fingers in her panties and gingerly dragged them down. His attention went to the soft curls as he slid the fabric off her foot, tossing them aside.

"Damn, New York, look at you." He pressed a kiss to her belly…her inner thigh…moving closer and closer to where her trembling told him she wanted him to go.

She threaded her fingers into his hair. "Please," she whispered.

Ravenous need stormed over him at her plea. But there was something more that he wanted. More than his own need. *Her taste.* Desperate to have all of this surprising woman who was changing him as a man, he glided his tongue against her. Her soft moan was the only sound he heard as he brought her to pleasure.

Over.

And over again.

Slowly. Carefully. Intently.

Until her breathing began hitching, her body shaking with the force of his tongue caressing her. But it wasn't enough. Not nearly enough. He added one finger into his affection. Then another.

Giving her more…taking her higher…and soon she broke apart around him, a beautiful mess of satisfaction, shuddering against his mouth.

He only backed away when her soft whimper brushed across him. She released the tight hold on his hair, so he pressed a final kiss to her thigh and rose. Her half-lidded eyes held his as he gathered her in his arms and laid her out on the bed. Her legs were parted, cheeks and chest flushed beautifully, an invitation he wouldn't refuse.

Hastily, he retrieved his wallet from his pants, and as he reached for a condom, she took his hardened length into her hands.

"You're not the only one who wants to play," she rasped.

He grunted at the feel of her tight hand against him, tossing his head back before he forced himself to watch her have her fun. A rumbly growl rose from his chest at the playfulness in her eyes. He'd never known a woman who was bold, brave, sweet and shy all at once. The combination was devastatingly perfect. His perfect woman, one he never knew he wanted or needed.

She was wreaking havoc on his control.

His legs began trembling, pleasure rushing through his veins with the frantic beat of his heart. When tension rushed up his spine, he stepped free, breaking her hold. Throbbing and on the brink of losing it, he growled, "...e only way we end tonight is with me inside you."

"Then get over here," she said, grinning, sliding far-ther back on the bed.

Eager to feel her, he sheathed himself in a condom and then joined her on the soft mattress that bounced under his weight. He blanketed his body over her, pull-ing one of her thighs back as he went. A beauty beneath him, he sealed his mouth across hers and primed him-self at her entrance.

Then he pushed forward, entering her halfway. Though he was nearly seeing stars at the pleasure sky-rocketing through him, her tight kiss told him to wait.

She gasped against his lips, "Colter."

"Yeah, New York, you're going to take all of me." He sealed his mouth across hers again, deepening the kiss. He slowly pumped his hips, relishing her wet warmth and hold. He broke away, kissing her jawline. "I've wanted this from the moment I saw you."

"Me, too." She moaned as he thrust forward slightly, moving in deeper.

Again.

And again.

Until he groaned against her neck, seated all the way to the hilt. He nipped at her neck, and her eager moan lifted his attention. She panted with urgency, so he low-ered his mouth to hers and kissed her. Deeper. Harder.

Until she whimpered, wiggling beneath him, meeting him thrust for thrust.

Right there, taken by pleasure alongside her, he began moving gently, slowly.

Her moans traveled like wildfire across his flesh as he kissed all the exposed parts of her. She arched back when he latched onto a nipple, so he sucked hard. Nibbled the hard peak until her moans turned raspy. Desperate.

She grabbed his bottom, locking her ankles around his thighs, and he let go of his restraint. Giving them what they both wanted, he rode her hard, fast, each thrust building until their minds were stolen and over-whelmed by pleasure.

Skin slapped against skin. The smell of their sex infusing the air. She became too much. All of her. The greatness of her. The feel of her. He broke the kiss, needing to watch her fall apart in his arms. Though nothing prepared him for the emotions battering his chest when he looked deep into her eyes. Her guard was down, her soul right there for the taking, and damn, did he want to claim her.

Any control he might have had was currently stripped away. His movements became frantic as her screams begged him to finish her.

He stared into her beautiful pleasure until the very last moment. Only then did he dare shut his eyes and lose himself to sensation, hearing her final scream of satisfaction as she followed him over the edge.

"Oh, hell, yes, girl. *Get it*," Nora said through the phone line as Adeline sank down on the closed toilet seat.

In the white marble bathroom, with gold accents on just about everything and rich floral scents from the potpourri infusing the air, Adeline pressed her cell phone to her ear, keeping the conversation private. "This isn't a huge mistake?" she asked.

Nora scoffed. "Um, no, sleeping with that hella sexy cowboy is the best decision you've ever made. Why are you even questioning this?"

"Because I feel like somehow in all this, our fake relationship, fake engagement, whatever you want to call it, nothing is fake anymore."

"Would that be such a bad thing?"

"I don't know," Adeline answered honestly, staring at the all-glass shower across the bathroom. "It's just messed up. I mean, who breaks off her engagement and then suddenly gets with someone else?"

"Lots of people," Nora said. "Besides, Brock cheated on you. It's not like you don't have a good reason to move on with your life. You've had a crush on Colter for forever. You deserve to have a little fun."

Adeline nearly didn't respond but knew that would get her nowhere. "Yeah, but that's what you don't get, Nora. Colter isn't a guy you just have fun with. He's incredible. He's so good to his family, his community—even to me."

Nora hesitated, a long, obvious pause. "You're catching feelings?"

"Catching them?" Adeline laughed. "I've had feelings for him since high school. And now he's this grown man who's—" she stared at the closed bathroom door—to Colter on the other side "—just perfect in every way. God, Nora, he's my dream guy. In bed and out of it."

"I'm not really seeing the problem here," Nora mused.

Adeline huffed, rising and moving in front of the mirror. She wore a white hotel robe. Her makeup was smudged beneath her eyes, her hair messy, satisfaction glistening in her glossy eyes. "It's just confusing, because none of this was supposed to happen. I came here to write a story, and now everything is all over the place and I'm wondering what in the hell I'm doing here."

"What do you mean, *everything*?"

Adeline moved to the large soaker tub and sat on the edge. "My dad…this town…it's getting in my head."

"Have you seen your dad again?"

"No," Adeline said, pressing her toes against the cool marble floors. "It's just weird. I'm around Colter's family all the time and they are just so close, it's making me feel like something is missing in life, even though I have you and my mom, which has always been enough."

"I think you're forgetting your father is not like Colter's family. He wasn't there for you at all."

"I haven't forgotten," Adeline confirmed. Then she gave her head a good hard shake. "Like I said, everything is just…getting confusing."

"Well, I don't really know what to say about your dad but to say be careful. He's not going to care about your heart, so protect yourself."

"Yeah, probably best."

Nora paused again, obviously considering what Adeline had told her. "Here's what I do know. Two men in your life have been utter disappointments. It sucks. The only thing you can do is control how you respond to them. And I say, when you finally meet a guy who is everything you have ever wanted and then some, you'd be insane not to act on it."

"Even if he lives in a small town that I'd never move back to."

"Even if," Nora said. "Maybe this is your shot at true, lasting love. When it's that kind of love, it'll work out. It always does."

"So don't shut this down is what you're saying?"

"Yes. Let things go where they want to go. Either something will come of it or you'll come home with an amazing story of how you had two hot weeks with your biggest crush."

Adeline smiled, a sudden weight lifting off her shoulders. "That is quite the story."

"It is. Now get back out there and enjoy that cowboy."

"Yes, ma'am," Adeline said before adding, "I love you, Nora. Thanks for listening."

"You'd do the same for me. Love you, babe. Talk soon."

The phone line went dead, and Adeline left her cell phone by the sink, hearing a knock on the hotel room's door. She waited for the door to open, and when she came out of the bathroom, she found Colter shutting the door, a tray in his hand, wearing a robe matching hers.

"Snacks," he said, pulling off the silver lid, revealing fruit and almond butter.

"Yum." She joined him on the king bed with its white duvet and wall of pillows, sitting cross-legged. He placed the tray down in front of her and then slid on his side as she remarked, "You do realize we broke our own rules."

"Yup, and I don't give a shit," Colter replied, tossing a piece of apple into his mouth.

"Until you do give a shit," she said, reaching for an apple and dipping it into the almond butter.

He froze midway to picking up another apple and arched an eyebrow. "Explain what that means."

"I just mean, isn't this exactly what you didn't want? We fake dated so that you could get women away from you."

"That's different," he said.

"How?"

He winked. "Because I like you."

Her insides turned to mush, but she didn't get the chance to reply as he dipped the apple in the almond butter and then lifted it to her mouth.

His voice lowered as she took a bite. "I knew there was something special about you the moment you walked into the bar."

"Oh?" she asked. "Special how?"

He dragged the apple across her lips. "I liked the way you looked at me. Not like a prize. Like a man." He hesitated, eating the remainder of the apple. She licked the sweet flavor off her lips as he continued, "More than that—you didn't look at me like I was broken."

She lifted her brows. "People think *you're* broken?"

He grinned, tapping her nose. "See, that surprises you. I like that."

"No, seriously, though, who would think that?" she countered, snagging another apple and dipping it in the butter before taking a nibble. "You honestly seem like the most put-together guy I know."

"If you'd come here six months ago, you would have thought very different."

"Because of the divorce?"

He nodded. "At the time, I felt like I'd failed my family for leaving them in the first place. I felt like I failed to hold my marriage together. I felt like, in every aspect of my life, I failed. I didn't come home in a good place."

"You were heartbroken," she said gently.

"Terribly. I drank too much, refused to talk to anyone and worked too damn hard. I was pretty miserable to be around."

Laughter and footsteps sounded outside their door before fading away. "What changed all that?"

He hesitated and visibly swallowed, pain evident in his voice and on his face. "My dad came to the house one night. He wasn't in a wheelchair then, but he knew his body was failing him. He gave me an out on running the ranch. He told me I could return to flying, because he'd hired a CEO to fill his role."

She took his hand, hoping somehow that eased the obvious hurt he felt at the memory, as he continued, "He looked me in the eye, man to man, and in the darkest days of his life, probably hating to even ask, he thought of me and of my happiness."

"So, then you thought of him and got better?" she guessed.

He ran his thumb over the back of her hand, his attention remaining there. "Exactly." When his head lifted again, his gaze was filled with warmth. "It made me see that I needed to get over myself, because what I was going through was nothing in comparison to him. I promised him that day that I'd shape up."

"And you did?"

He nodded, proud. "I did."

Gosh, to just *change* for the better. She envied his ability to do that so easily.

He ran a finger along her jawline, drawing her out of her thoughts. "What's that look all about?"

"I wish I could do what you did," she admitted. "Hell, I'm still wondering how I nearly married someone who was cheating on me."

"Cruel people are very good actors."

She shrugged. "I guess, but I honestly just don't know how to pick up and move on like you did. I know that, soon, I'll have to go home and face Brock and his family, and I'm not sure how I'll do that."

"Finding strength in heartbreak didn't happen overnight," he said, adamant. "It took me six months of punishing myself to get there."

"Oh, great. Is that what I have to look forward to?"

He suddenly moved the tray out of the way and grabbed her leg, pulling her toward him. She let out a squeal as he hovered over her. "You'll never go to that dark place, because your sweet, sunny heart simply couldn't." He pulled the tie on her robe until it fell open, then kissed her neck, her breast, her stomach.

She threaded her hands through his hair as his kisses continued lower, setting her on fire. "I thought you said you were hungry."

"I am," he said, pressing a kiss to her inner thigh before moving closer to where she wanted him. "But I'm just hungry for something else now."

"Oh, yeah, what's that?" she rasped playfully.

"You." His tongue met her heated flesh.

As she arched off the mattress falling into the pleasure, she realized Nora was right—this was the best decision she'd ever made.

Nine

Four days later, Adeline was living on an orgasmic high. Every minute of every day she'd spent with Colter had seemed better than the one before it. She'd spent her mornings shadowing him at work for her story and the afternoons writing what she'd learned about Colter with Waylon.

She'd finished her article two days ago, but the article was the furthest thing from her mind. First, she didn't feel like writing about Colter anymore—she felt like experiencing him for real. Second, in just two short days, she'd leave Colter and Devil's Bluffs behind.

The thought seemed nearly impossible. She'd never felt such hunger for any man. Such desire, like she never could get enough of him. No matter how many times she and Colter had fallen apart in each other's arms—in the morning, afternoon, at night, whenever they could—she wanted *more*.

But her bigger problem? Her heart was reaching for things with Colter that complicated everything. Because she knew if Colter lived in New York City, she'd keep dating him without question, without hesitation, regardless that she was fresh off a breakup. Things with Colter were good...*too good*.

A thought she desperately tried to push away as she slid into cowboy boots she'd borrowed from Colter's mother. They pinched at the ankles, but sore feet were the least of her worries.

Horseshoes clicking against the driveway drew her gaze up. Colter approached with two horses, tacked up and ready to ride, and she gulped. *Yup, terrible idea.*

"Regretting saying yes to a ride?" Colter asked, smirking.

"A little," she admitted.

"You've really never ridden before?" Beverly asked, swinging back and forth in the rocking chair on the farmhouse's porch.

"Never in my life," she answered.

"You're a Texan," Colter rebuked, stopping at the porch and shaking his head in disapproval. "That's a travesty."

Adeline slid the borrowed tan-colored cowboy hat onto her head and rose. "A Texan who lived near town and who only set foot on a farm when I babysat Beau."

"We should have had the boys take you," Beverly stated. "Shame on us. Isn't that right, Grant?" She patted her husband's hand.

Where he sat in his wheelchair, Grant's eyes were glazed over today. He stared off at the barn, mumbling words no one could decipher.

Adeline wasn't sure whom to feel worse for—Grant, since the last few days had not been easy on him. She could hardly believe how much frailer he looked in such a short time. Or Beverly, Colter and Beau, who all suffered right alongside him. She'd never seen Parkinson's up close and personal before. She'd had no idea how cruel the disease was, or that dementia came into play with Parkinson's and how fast it stole someone away.

When Grant didn't acknowledge them, still staring off at the barn, mumbling, Beverly patted his hand. "Exactly. We did Adeline wrong." To Adeline, she added, "It's good Colter's rectifying this."

"Let's hope so," Adeline muttered, trotting down the porch steps. "I may actually die in the process."

"I'd never let that happen," Colter said, tapping the rim of her cowboy hat.

She felt marginally better.

In quick work, Colter gave her a leg up and she was hoisted atop the white horse. He adjusted her stirrups and then mounted his black horse as easily as she climbed a set of stairs.

"Enjoy yourselves," Beverly said as they rode off.

"Thanks," Adeline called before studying the way Colter held his reins in one hand. She did the same and asked, "What do I need to know here?"

"Squeeze your legs to go faster. Give a little tug on the reins to stop and say *whoa*. Not much more than that. Just go nice and easy." He gestured to the horse.

"Pearl will take good care of you. Just relax into the saddle and enjoy the ride."

"Okay," she said hesitantly. Pearl was massive and powerful, but Colter looked relaxed, so she followed his advice.

They passed the barn, where cowboys were busy working. Pearl followed Colter's horse up the small hill along a dirt trail until they entered a flat pasture. Her horse seemed to know what she was doing, so Adeline rested one hand on her leg, the other holding the reins on the horn of the saddle.

As they headed deeper into the meadow, surrounded by lush vegetation and rolling hills, she studied the cowboy next to her. Colter's relaxed shoulders. His lax expression. He looked the same when he flew—at home and most comfortable.

She was beginning to feel the same way, too.

The days she'd spent back in Devil's Bluffs had left her breathless. The sex had been the greatest of her life. Each day that passed only seemed to sizzle more. She couldn't fool herself—she was happy. Probably the happiest she'd been in a very long time. She wished more than ever that this relationship wouldn't end in two days. She was not only spending more time with Colter than she ever had with Brock, and she was happy to do so, but she wondered if this was what a healthy relationship looked like.

Quiet. Comfortable. Easy.

"My dad was looking rough, huh?" asked Colter, breaking the silence.

She noted the tension in his eyes. "A little, yeah. It's very sad."

He gave a slow nod, then set his troubled gaze back on the view ahead of him. "My mom was telling me this morning that it's the recommendation of the nursing home that he doesn't leave the property anymore. It's too much for him."

"I'm sorry, Colter," she said, wishing she could reach for him. "I can't imagine how hard that must be for all of you."

"I'm most sorry for my mother" was all he said.

Her heart broke for Beverly, too. Pearl grabbed a mouthful of grass before quickening her walk to catch up to Colter's horse. "Is that why you left a job you loved and came home? For your mother?"

He glanced at her sidelong, heaviness in his stare. "Family stands above all. They needed me. It wasn't even a question if I'd come home."

"Even if it meant giving up your dream job?"

"Even if."

Pearl suddenly tripped a little before she righted herself. Once Adeline knew she wasn't about to hit the dirt, she added, "You're a good man, you know, giving up your dreams and desires to make sure your family is happy. Not everyone would do that."

He watched her closely. Then heaved a sigh. "If I learned anything from what's happening with my father, it's that at the end of your life, it's not money with you or a dream job—it's your memories and your loved ones."

She smiled but couldn't take her eyes off him. Behind his tough, cool-guy persona was a man with strong morals, a family man, and one who selflessly put his own wishes and dreams aside to do right by his family.

Dear God, he was her dream come true.

"I envy the relationship you have with your family," she admitted, the morning sun beating down on her. "The way you guys are there for each other. I can only imagine what your Christmases must be like. Is it as magical as I think it would be?"

"It's pretty magical," Colter agreed with a laugh. "My mom really goes all out. You didn't have that with your mom?"

"Oh, I did," she countered. "My mom is amazing and always did what she could to make every day magical for me, but I just mean, having family. Brothers…a dad… that kind of thing."

A long pause followed. Then, "Have you really not wanted to meet your dad?"

She hesitated now, touching on that sore spot to see if she could talk about it. She was relieved to find it didn't hurt like it used to. "My mom only told me his name when I turned sixteen, and I think she only told me that because she never expected me to come back here."

"Was she protecting you?"

"I think so." She nodded. "My dad never wanted children. When my mother told him she was pregnant, he was clear about his views on becoming a father. My mom said he was a big drinker. She decided it'd be better for me not to be involved with him, and he thought it better, too."

He cocked his head. "What do you think of that?"

"You mean, do I think it was honorable he stayed out of my life, knowing he'd be a bad father?"

Colter nodded, resting his hand on the horn of his saddle.

She looked away to give Pearl's neck a stroke, her mane gorgeously long and flowing. "It took me a long time to see the good in what he'd done—" she glanced his way again "—but yes, I do think it's honorable that he stayed away if he knew he'd be a terrible father. But I guess it kind of makes me sad, too."

"Why sad?"

"It makes me wonder what happened to him that he wouldn't choose more love in his life."

A sweet smile crossed Colter's face as an eagle shrieked above, soaring through the air. "You've got a big heart, Adeline."

"Probably a bad thing, really."

"How can *that* be a bad thing?"

The wind rustled the long grass as Pearl snatched another mouthful. "Because it puts you in situations where you get hurt. Trust me, I've got the bruises to show for it."

A long pause followed as Colter frowned. He finally asked, "Does your father still live in town?"

"He does, yes," she explained. "I actually saw him when I first arrived. Remember when you found me on the ground?"

His mouth twitched. "When you fell, right?"

She snorted. "Fell into a bush to avoid my dad seeing me."

Awareness touched Colter's face. "Ah, that makes more sense. Do you think he saw you?"

She shrugged. "Honestly, I doubt he'd even recognize me. Why would he? I'm a perfect stranger to him."

"I cannot understand how a man could do that to his

daughter," Colter said gruffly. Though his voice softened when he asked, "Can I ask who your father is?"

She hesitated but then realized she shouldn't have. She wanted Colter to know her. "He's Eric Lowe."

Colter's brows shot up. "From Lowe's Mechanics?"

"That'd be the one," she said, shifting her hips with Pearl's rhythm.

"Jesus," Colter snapped. "He works on all our trucks for us."

"Whatever you do, please don't change that," she countered. "I don't want it to be weird for him or anything." When she saw the vein protruding in the middle of Colter's forehead, she hastily added, "Really, Colter, I didn't tell you to make a fuss. Just being honest."

He tore his gaze away, his glare burning up the tree line ahead of him. "All right," he eventually said calmly. "I won't make a fuss. Do you plan on going to see him while you're here?"

"See him?" She pondered the thought. "No, I've got nothing to say to him. What would I even ask?"

His glare returned and burned. "Not a damn thing, but you could show him how amazing you are and that his failures didn't break you."

Her heart squeezed in all the right ways. "Thank you for saying that."

"I'm only saying what's true," he said gently. Then he rubbed the scruff on his chin. "I never would have guessed he's a drunk."

"Maybe he's just good at hiding it."

"Maybe," Colter agreed.

A comfortable quiet settled in, and Adeline didn't

feel the need to fill it. There was a certain peace to riding a horse in nature. She made a mental note to add this experience to her article—to discuss how both the Ward sons were very easygoing and laid-back people—when suddenly Colter stopped his horse. Adeline's automatically stopped, too.

He met her with a soft expression. "There are three things I know for certain. One, your father made the biggest mistake by not having you in his life. Two, if you change your mind and you want to meet him, I'll be there with you, by your side."

Her heart skipped at the idea of meeting Eric Lowe. She'd never considered it. Didn't see the point of it, but now, after being around the Wards, she couldn't help but wonder if perhaps she was missing out. Maybe her father did regret not knowing her... "And three?" she asked, curious.

He grinned from ear to ear. "I've got a killer right hook that I'd be glad to introduce him to, if that suits you."

She barked an unexpected laugh. "Thanks. I'll certainly keep that in mind."

Later that night, in Beau's rustic kitchen with its oak cabinets and dark quartz countertops, Colter nudged a wood block carefully out of the Jenga tower, which began to wobble before the blocks crashed to the live edge table.

Sitting across from him, Austin screamed in joy, jumping up. He high-fived Adeline. "We got him," his nephew exclaimed.

"We sure did," she said with a laugh.

Austin bounced in his chair. "Can we play again?"

"Sorry, buddy, it's bedtime." Colter rose, pushing his chair under the table. "You're already up later than you should be."

"But…but…"

"Your dad will have my hide," Colter reminded his nephew. He wasn't sure what time Beau would get home after his date with a woman Riggs had introduced him to at the Black Horse, but he wasn't taking chances with his brother giving him grief. "Neither of us wants to deal with that."

Austin's shoulders slumped, but he eventually perked up again, remembered his manners. Beaming at Adeline, he said, "Thanks for babysitting me."

"I had so much fun," she told him, restacking the blocks until the tower was built again. "Next time, we'll kick Uncle Colter's butt playing Monopoly."

Colter's jaw clenched against the awareness that hit her expression the second her mouth shut. There would not be a next time. Soon, she'd be back in New York City and returning to her life there.

Austin didn't know that. "Oh, yeah, totally kick his butt," Austin said, smiling, before taking off down the hall.

"You shouldn't encourage him," Colter told her with a smile.

She held up her hands in surrender. "But you make it so easy."

"Ha-ha," he said with a snort, following Austin down the hallway and into his bedroom. "Pj's on and brush your teeth, buddy."

"On it," said Austin, and in a flurry, he grabbed pajamas from the drawer, spun on his heels and headed off to the bathroom.

By the time Colter pulled the patchwork quilt back on the bed and turned off the bedroom's light, the night-light giving off slight, warm light, Austin was jumping into bed. "All set?" Colter asked, tucking him in.

"Yup." Austin turned onto his side, snuggling into the pillow.

Colter missed reading a book to Austin at bedtime but had been firmly told by his nephew that he was too old for that now. "Sleep well, little man." Colter tousled his nephew's hair.

When he went to turn away, Austin asked, "Can Adeline come over tomorrow to play Monopoly?"

"Sorry, bud, but I think she's busy."

Austin pouted. "When can she come, then?"

Colter hesitated, the question suddenly seeming daunting. He took a seat on the side of the bed and explained gently, "I don't think she can. She's heading back home to New York City soon, where she lives."

"Can't she move here?"

Such an innocent question, from an innocent kid. "That's a hard thing for adults to do sometimes."

"Doesn't seem so hard," Austin muttered. "Just pack her stuff in boxes and bring it here."

Colter tousled his nephew's hair again. He wished that was the case. Every day that passed seemed to get better than the one before it. Things with Adeline were easy, hot and spectacular. Were she not leaving, he'd believe he was in the beginning of an incredible relationship that was only getting better as the days passed. "Believe me, if I could have her move here, I would."

"Then ask her," Austin said.

Feeling like the kid was smarter than he was, Colter rose and moved to the door. "I'll think about it. It's time for sleep. 'Night, buddy."

"'Night."

Colter headed out the door, leaving it open a crack just as Austin liked it. He heard Adeline's laugh followed by Beau's on his way back to the kitchen.

When he reentered the kitchen, he found Beau leaning against the kitchen counter while Adeline still sat at the table. She'd packed the game back into the box. "You're home early," he said to his brother.

Beau looked at his watch before arching an eyebrow. "A little late for bed, don't you think?"

Colter shrugged. "Better late than never."

Beau snorted a laugh, folding his arms. "As for being home early, I'm not sure I could have taken more." He sighed. "I spent an hour learning about everything her ex-husband did wrong."

"That good, huh?" Colter snorted, sidling up to Adeline, wrapping his hands around the back of the chair.

"Worse than you could even imagine," his brother grumbled. To Adeline, he asked, "Can you make a photograph of me go viral? I could use the help in finding a woman."

"I wish, but sorry, I'm not that good," Adeline said, grinning, rising from the table. "Austin and I did kick Colter's butt a few times playing Jenga, so at least the night wasn't a total waste."

"At least there is that." Beau winked.

Colter huffed, moving to the door and picking up his Stetson from the hook. "We better get on our way before you two team up on me and somehow I end up losing more tonight."

"What a chicken," Beau called after him.

Adeline laughed, and Colter gathered her close in his arms. "You think that's funny, huh?"

Her eyes twinkled as she melted beautifully against him. "Extremely."

He'd never yearned to keep anything, but he wanted to keep Adeline. Close. Just like this. For as long as she'd let him. It'd been a year since he'd dated anyone. What started out as fake was certainly not that now. Days of happiness had erased that line, but questions kept echoing in his mind. Why did he have to meet her now? Why couldn't he have seen her back in high school? Why did she have to live in the damn city?

His body vibrated with his need to keep her with him. But he wasn't sure if he could convince her to stay. He knew why he'd asked about her father, why he'd pressed the matter—he was desperate to remove her obstacles so she could see Devil's Bluffs as home again.

Gently, he pressed a kiss to her forehead. "You're both traitors." He opened the door to their continued laughter. Then said to his brother, "Sorry about the date."

Beau shrugged, moving toward them. "A night out is a night out. Thanks for entertaining Austin."

"He's a real cutie," Adeline said, stepping outside.

Out of sight of Adeline, Beau mouthed, *She's a keeper.*

Colter nodded agreement and then joined Adeline outside. They said a quick goodbye to Beau and hit the road a few minutes later. The beams of Colter's headlights lit up the dark, windy road as he drove in the opposite direction from his house. Adeline didn't seem to notice they weren't going home until he left Ward land behind and slowed down in front of the high school.

When he turned into the driveway, she asked, "What are we doing here?"

Colter parked the truck. "Fulfilling a fantasy."

"What are you talking about?" she said with a laugh, following him outside.

He met her at the hood and took her hand, leading her toward the football field. Memories flooded him. Good ones. When life was easy and fun and he'd thought happiness was a right given to anyone. Now, of course, he knew better and knew that happiness came from hard work. Both in relationships and out of them.

Once they reached the football field, a quiet, dark, still night around him, he moved to the bleachers, not seeing anyone that would interrupt his plans for the evening.

She slowly moved closer to him, giving a sexy smile. "You can't be serious."

"Oh, I'm very serious," he said, tugging her into him. "Tell me what you thought about when you saw me at school and were crushing hard." He slid his hand down to cup her bottom, bringing her up against him. "Did you think about me doing this to you? Bringing you closer?"

"Yes," she rasped.

He dragged his nose against hers. "Did you think about my mouth?"

"Yes."

He sealed his mouth over hers and kissed her passionately. "Like this? This is what you wanted?"

"Yes, I wanted you to kiss me." She hesitated before rasping, "But there was something else I always wanted to do to you."

"What was that?"

Her smile tightened his groin. He went hard as steel as she lowered to her knees and reached for his belt.

He arched an eyebrow at her. "*That* is what you thought about doing to me?"

She nodded slowly, nibbling her lip. "Touching you. Tasting you. Yes, it's all I thought about." She got his belt open and began unzipping his fly. "And all I'm thinking about now."

A rough laugh escaped him. "You and I would have gotten along very well back then, New York."

Her eyes shined as she opened the front of his pants and slid them down enough that his cock sprang free. "Really? So, you would have liked this?" She licked up the length of him.

He threw his head back and groaned as she took him deep into her mouth, her hand following behind. "Christ. Yes."

He couldn't think, focus, do anything at all but feel every bit of her silky tongue and wet mouth as she brought his soul into her hands. Every move was skilled, like she had the playbook on how to drive him wild.

Until he felt the tremors rock him, the heat shooting

up his spine. One look down at her head bobbing on him and he was a near goner.

He reached for her before she could finish him. He spun her around until she was pressed against the bleachers. "Stay there for me, New York." He took a condom from his wallet and hastily sheathed himself.

He couldn't take his eyes off her as he reached around, unbuttoning her jeans and shoving them just down past her bottom. The need to claim her—and to keep her right there with him and give this thing between them a real shot—overtook him as he stepped in close behind her. He slid his hand between her thighs, finding her ready, and he didn't need more of an invitation.

Her heady moans echoed around him as he positioned himself at her entrance. With a growl, he gripped her hip and entered her in one swift stroke.

Her shout of ecstasy brushed across his senses. That was all it took to drive him wild and eliminate any sense of control.

This time, he didn't go slow and easy.

This time, he held her hips, pinned her against the bleachers and rode her hard, commanding her body. Their moans blended, their jagged breathing uniting in the roughness of the pleasure.

Until her inner walls squeezed him tight, her scream of release satisfying something primal deep inside him. Only then—when she was screaming his name—did he follow her, roaring, bucking and jerking against her, wishing every single day for the rest of his life could be this good.

Ten

"How's engaged life?" Riggs asked the following day in the Black Horse.

Sitting across from him in a booth, Colter replied against the rim of his beer bottle, wet with condensation, "Hilarious." He'd had a busy morning at the ranch with a couple of sick cattle but made time for lunch with Riggs. He swallowed the beer, the taste of hops and spices lingering on his tongue, and then set the bottle down on the table. A little too firmly, judging from Riggs's raised brows.

"That good, huh?" Riggs asked.

"Actually, it's too good," Colter admitted to his childhood friend. "It's so good that it's easy to forget all this happened because of a fake relationship."

Riggs shook his head slowly. "What a situation to be in."

Colter agreed with a nod. "It's been…*interesting*." He felt all his guards fall in the comfort of his friend's presence. Riggs had been there for him when he'd come home after his divorce, broken. Whenever Colter needed an ear, Riggs listened. "Listen, I'm sorry I haven't been around much."

"Ah, don't be sorry," Riggs countered, straightening the cardboard menu stand on the table. "She's making you happy. Nothing beats that. How much longer is Adeline here?"

The bartender behind the bar—must be a new employee, since Colter hadn't met him—filled an order from a chatty patron sitting on the stool. The very stool Colter had been sitting on the day Adeline uprooted his life for the better. "She's set to fly home tomorrow morning."

Riggs frowned. "That soon, huh?"

"Too soon." Two weeks was all he had with her. But those weeks had been the best he'd had in a very long time. Fourteen days with her was not enough time.

Riggs sipped his malt scotch, the ice clanging in his glass. "Have you seen the article she's written about you?"

"Not yet." Colter hesitated. "Not sure I want to. If it's finished, it'll mean she's going back to New York City."

"Obviously not something you want."

Riggs knew Colter. Truly. He'd been his friend the longest. His greatest ally. "She is the greatest thing to happen to me. Is it insane of me to hope she doesn't write the article? That she decides she wants to live the story with me instead of heading back to the city?"

"No, it isn't insane," Riggs said after a moment of consideration. "But it's a big ask."

"Yeah, it is," Colter agreed, picking at the label on his beer. "Doesn't mean I don't want to ask it. The very last thing I want right now is for her to go home. Things are good. Better than they've been in so damn long."

Riggs cocked his head. "Have you asked her if she feels the same way?"

Colter snorted. "Not sure I want to know her answer." She liked him, that he knew. She was happy... and *satisfied*, that he also knew. He had finally found a woman he could see himself getting serious with again. But the obstacles stopping them from being together were there, and there was nothing Colter could do to remove them. She was heartbroken. Devil's Bluffs was not her home.

Frustration cut through him as he carved a hand through his hair. "She's *just* coming off a heartbreak. A big one—that I know for certain she has not dealt with."

"Maybe she doesn't need to deal with it," Riggs offered. "Not everyone deals with things the same way. If you ask me, you should man up and ask her to stay. You deserve happiness. Choose that."

Cheering from a table across from them grabbed Colter's attention. On the flat-screen television on the wall, a Professional Bull Riding event had just gotten underway. That explained why, even at midday, the bar was packed. He smiled at Riggs. "Thanks. Appreciate that. How are things with you?"

"Can't complain," Riggs said with a slight shrug. "Bar's doing well. Nightmares are staying away—" Colter knew

Riggs's sleep was often disturbed by PTSD "—and the ladies are coming in plenty."

"Literally?" Colter asked.

Riggs barked a laugh. "Of course, man, of course." He took another sip of his drink before adding, "We should get a poker night going."

Damn, it'd been weeks since they had one. They usually got together at least weekly. "I'll get a call into the ranch to see who wants to join," Colter said. Beau would want in, as he usually did, and a few of the cowboys always joined, too.

He went to grab his beer when his phone beeped in his pocket. One look at the screen, and he smiled. *Adeline.*

Her text read, Can I see you?

He fired off a text back. Sure, I'm at the Black Horse. Meet me here.

Her response popped up a moment later. I'm just at the coffee shop. Be there in a few.

"What's up?" Riggs asked.

"Adeline's coming by in a couple minutes." He tucked his phone back into his pocket. "I'm glad we could do this."

"Me, too." Riggs slapped a hand on the table. "And it's good to see a woman making you smile from a text alone. She must be some woman."

Colter smiled. "She is."

True to her word, Adeline arrived at the bar a few minutes later, after Colter had already settled his bill. She strode past the patrons, garnering looks from the men there. Colter leaned back against the booth, taking his fill of her as she approached.

Damn.

Her silky blouse clung against all her incredible curves. The tight black pants and heels were just begging to hit his bedroom floor. But more than the lust alone driving him, his chest warmed whenever she came near.

Her eyes twinkled with heat, as if she could read his thoughts. "Hi," she said when she sidled up to the table. She stuck her hand out. "Riggs, right?"

Riggs gave her his charming smile that all the ladies loved. He took her hand and shook it gently. "That'd be me, and you must be Adeline."

"You got it. It's really nice to meet you." She studied the empty plates, with only chicken wing sauce and bones, on the table. "Sorry, am I interrupting?"

"Not at all," Riggs said, sliding out of the booth. "We're all done here, and I gotta head back to work anyway." He gathered up all the plates, as well as Colter's empty beer bottle and his glass. "Can I grab you a drink, food, anything?"

"No, thanks, I'm okay," she replied.

Colter gestured her into Riggs's seat, and she took his spot as Colter said to Riggs, "I'll be in touch about that poker game."

"Sounds good to me," Riggs said before setting that charming smile back onto Adeline. "Again, nice to meet you, Adeline."

"You, too. Hope to see you soon."

Colter gritted his teeth, beginning to hate that line.

Because she wouldn't see him again. She was leaving tomorrow morning. Unless he could think of a way to convince her that staying with him would be the best decision of her life.

Riggs turned away but not before waggling his eyebrows in obvious approval over Adeline. Colter couldn't agree more.

He focused back on Adeline, taking note of her wringing hands. A jolt shot through his limbs at the unease on her face. "Everything okay?" he asked, hoping she was changing her mind about leaving.

"Sort of," she said. "I mean, kind of."

He arched a single eyebrow at her.

She laughed nervously. "Okay, I guess that makes no sense at all. You see, this morning I was talking to Nora about everything that has happened, and how I'm feeling about stuff…and…"

Colter hung on bated breath, waiting for her next words to make him a very happy man. But she surprised him.

"I actually have a big favor to ask," she said.

"Of course. Whatever you need. What's going on?"

She rubbed the back of her neck, visibly swallowing. "Can I still take you up on your offer to come with me to meet my dad?"

Of all the things he'd been expecting her to ask, that wasn't it. He reached for her shaky hands, taking them in his. "Are you sure you want to do that?" He wasn't sure he wanted her to meet the bastard who had turned his back on his own child.

She pondered for a moment. Then nodded firmly. "I

keep going back and forth, to be honest. Do I want this? Do I not? But in the end, after talking to Nora, and after our talk about him, I feel like this is my one and only chance to meet him. To find out what happened from his side of things. To understand what went so wrong with him that he could turn his back on a child."

She hesitated and drew in a deep breath. "I want him to see me. See that I'm doing well. And, if I'm honest, maybe I'm hoping a little that I can alleviate any guilt he has for being absent in my life. Maybe it could help his alcoholism."

Christ, this woman amazed him. He paused to consider what he'd heard. He couldn't help but hope that maybe—just maybe—she was trying to make her life better in Devil's Bluffs for herself. That she was also thinking of the future and how she could make things good here. Or at least doable so she didn't have to leave at all. Maybe, just maybe, they could somehow make this work.

Feeling desperate to keep her there, and safe, he held her hands tight. "If you need answers, then let's get them."

Cheers erupted again from the other table as she smiled. "Thank you. I'm not sure I could do this alone."

"You could do this alone," he said, brushing his thumbs against her soft skin. "But I'm glad you asked me." He hesitated, thinking of her father. From what he knew of the man, he was decent enough. Although Colter didn't know Eric's history. "What if he disappoints you today?" he asked, throwing that out there.

"I've considered that," she said. "And, to be honest,

I'm not sure how I'll feel about it all. I just know that I don't want another day to pass without at least seeing him face-to-face." She hesitated. Then her voice strengthened. "I don't want to be the person hiding behind bushes to avoid him. I want to face him."

"Then we go," Colter said immediately.

She inhaled sharply, then slid out of the booth. "It's probably best if we go now, so I don't realize this is a huge mistake and I change my mind."

"You *can* change your mind, you know," he told her.

"No—" she lifted her chin "—I really can't. I need these answers."

The drive across town to Lowe's Mechanics took fifteen minutes, though it felt like a thousand had gone by. Sitting next to Colter in his truck, Adeline fidgeted the whole way while he took the roads easy. She wanted this. She *needed* this to look herself in the mirror every day. She refused to be that shy girl who was too afraid to speak up again. But her nerves didn't get that memo.

They drove past gorgeous mansions that sat high on hills. Farms' brands were on every metal gate leading up to million-dollar houses. Old money lived here in this part of Texas. Since she'd been there last, new mansions had seemed to pop up everywhere. The land belonging to the state now housed neighborhoods. Money was sprinkled everywhere on the land now.

Until they reached the small auto body shop on the corner of the road that had yet to have a millionaire take it over to knock it down. Her insides twisted. Eric's shop looked better than she had expected. The white paint was fresh, the garden cute, with big hostas filling up most of the space and brightly colored wildflowers occupying the rest.

Colter pulled into one of the parking spots in front of the shop and cut the ignition. He shifted in his seat, looking at her straight on. "You don't have to do this, you know." He placed a big, comforting hand on her thigh. "If you want to leave, we leave, no questions asked."

She studied the shop's sign, which likely glowed at night. Eric might not make millions, but his shop was well cared for, not quite the place she'd expected an alcoholic to own. Which only made her even more curious about the man. "Actually, I do need to do this," she said, tapping into a well of strength she hadn't known was there. "The other day when we talked about my dad, all I kept thinking was, maybe he's the reason I ended up with someone who eventually cheated on me. Maybe it isn't Brock I need to find peace with, it's my dad." Desperate to not change her mind, she opened the passenger door and got out. "It's time I find out what really happened from his side of things."

Colter removed the keys from the ignition and hopped out, joining her at the passenger side of his truck. "Want me to come with you?" he asked, his brow wrinkled.

Warmth flooded her as he took her hands, squeezing tight. "Thanks, but I need to do this alone."

"All right." He tugged her into him, wrapping his arms around her tight. His kiss gave her just the right amount of reassurance she needed. "You've got this," he said against her lips. "I'm here if you need me."

Oddly, she believed him on both fronts. It registered in

her mind how much she trusted Colter. How, even after Brock cheating, she believed every word this man said. Always. She liked his steadiness most. "Thank you. I appreciate that."

She gave his hands a final squeeze before releasing him. Digging deep into her well of strength, she left Colter behind and approached her father's shop. Both bays were open, with vehicles on lifts and ramps. Music played on the radio, barely audible over the sound of an electric drill.

"Excuse me," she called to the man working beneath the car. "I'm looking for Eric Lowe. Is he here?"

"Yeah, sorry, one moment," the man replied, moving out from beneath the car. When he began approaching, he wiped his hands on his oil-stained coveralls. His fingernails were rimmed with black grease. Her mind stuttered, taking in his brown hair with silver at the sides, round brown eyes and height, of over six feet.

"I'm Eric Lowe," her father said, frowning at something over her shoulder. "What can I do for you?"

Adeline followed his gaze, glancing over her shoulder. Colter leaned imposingly against his truck, glaring daggers at Eric. Her heart swelled with affection. Having someone in her corner felt good. *Real good.* Drawing in a deep breath to find her bravery, she faced her father. "I…I am—"

"Adeline," Eric wheezed, the color draining from his face. He took a wobbly step forward. "You're my daughter, aren't you?"

The ground rocked beneath her feet. "How did you know?" she managed.

Eric's gaze roamed her face. His voice shook. "You look just like your mother."

The unexpected softness in his eyes rocked her back on her heels. Tears welled in her eyes, and she cursed every single one. She dug her nails into her palms, letting the pain help her hide her emotions. She studied the hard lines of his face, every wrinkle, his dark eyes. "I certainly don't look anything like you."

"Not much like me, no, but your hair—" he visibly gulped, statue-still "—it's my mother's color." He glanced over her shoulder, scanning the area. "Is your mother here, too?"

"It's just me," Adeline answered. "I thought maybe I should come and meet you."

His eyes, full of dark shadows, widened. "That was brave of you. I'm glad you did. There's…things to say… things to explain."

She stared at this perfect stranger, not sure what she'd expected to find. But this soft-spoken, obviously hard-working man was not it. "I—"

"Daddy," a high-pitched voice squealed.

Adeline spun on her heels, spotting a young brown-haired girl, probably around ten years old, charging toward them.

The girl waved a paper in her hands. "I drew a painting!"

Behind her, a woman a bit younger than Adeline's mother's age strode toward them, holding hands with a little boy, who looked around seven years old.

"Oh, wow, look at that," Eric said, studying the picture of a cat sitting on top of a mushroom. "Just incredible, Sissy. You are quite the little artist."

"I am terribly sorry for interrupting," the woman, who must be Eric's wife, said to Adeline before guiding her daughter toward the shop. "Our daughter forgets that not everyone is as excited about her art as we are."

Adeline wanted to speak. She tried to, but nothing came out of her parted lips. A sour taste hit the back of her throat as she watched the woman plant a tender kiss on Eric's mouth, followed with Eric kissing the top of his son's head.

Adeline's world stopped turning, ice chilling her veins as the family chatted for a moment.

When they vanished into the office off the bay, Adeline barely managed, "You have a family?"

"I do, yes," Eric said, shoving his hands into his pockets. "A loving wife and two incredible kids."

Stepsiblings? *Family.* The air seemed to thin as Adeline fought to inhale. She gripped her stomach as it churned. "But how? You're an alcoholic. Not a family man."

Eric's shoulders hunched as he bowed his head, not meeting her gaze. "That is true," he said in a small voice. "I was an alcoholic for a long time. An ugly one. Even a terrible person, too." His head finally lifted, a flush creeping across his cheeks. "But I got help. I got better. And I changed my life."

No. No. No.

Her mind was scrambling to find a logical excuse for his actions. None of this made any sense. "If you changed for the better, why didn't you try and find me?"

A telephone rang off in the distance, but the sound seemed so far away as the realization dawned on her. "You didn't want me," she whispered.

He took a step forward, stare pained. "It's not like that."

She retreated a step. Of all the reasons she'd thought she didn't know her father, it had never occurred to her that he'd have a perfect family. One that she had dreamed of her entire life. A mom. A dad. Siblings.

She took another step back, an ache burning in the back of her throat. "This was a mistake. I shouldn't have come here."

"No, wait…" Eric reached out to her, his eyes wet. "Adeline, please…"

Even the wind seemed to go still as the pain of his betrayal ripped her apart. Turning, she ran toward Colter, who was already charging her way.

"Wait," Eric called.

Colter caught her in his arms and snarled, "Don't."

She heard her father skid to a halt behind her at the single powerful word growled from Colter's throat.

Her stomach rolled as Colter led her to the truck. She trembled as he opened the passenger-side door and she leaped inside. Everything went quiet; her heartbeat thundering in her ears no longer made a noise. She felt oddly sluggish. A hum filled the heavy silence, an emptiness invading all the warm spots inside.

Until she heard her father say, "Colter. Please. Just wait."

"I said, *don't*, Eric," Colter said through gritted teeth. Vaguely, she suddenly became aware they were driving again, but she couldn't recall Colter joining her in the truck or driving away from the shop. All she knew was Colter's strong, comforting hand on her thigh and that his strength was a pulsating force next to her. She stared out her window at a hawk soaring over the crops, wishing she could be that bird, that she could fly far, *far* away from here.

Eleven

A couple hours had gone by since they'd arrived home, and Adeline still hadn't come out of the guest room. Not that Colter blamed her—he'd been fighting against driving back to Eric's to take out his frustration on her father's face. He'd finished responding to the couple emails he'd needed to handle before he ended up in the kitchen and began cooking dinner.

Still, Adeline never came out of the room.

Goddamn you, Eric.

Colter never should have let the meeting happen. Because now the truth stared at him hard. Adeline wouldn't just want to leave Devil's Bluffs—she'd want to run and get on the first flight out of there.

Expelling a sigh to cut through the tension along his shoulders, he turned down the stove, letting the beef stroganoff simmer. He cleaned up the used dishes, setting the pot back onto the hanging rack above the island.

Time seemed to stand still when he knew she was in that room, crying. His house had never seemed emptier, quieter. The only sound came from the bubbling of the sauce on the stove, and his skin began to crawl.

Unable to stand the distance between them any longer, he moved down the hallway and stopped outside the guest room. He cocked his head, listening, but couldn't hear a single sound. Earlier when he'd walked by, he'd heard her on the phone—he figured to her mom or Nora.

He knocked once. "I've made dinner. Please come out. You must be hungry."

A long pause.

Again, he knocked. "Adeline?"

"I'll be out in a few minutes," she said, her voice sounding scratchy.

His fists clenched at the obvious tears she'd been crying. Yet again, he felt helpless to assist someone in his life. "I'll be in the kitchen," he told her before heading that way.

When he reached the stove again, picking up the wooden spoon off the banged-up cutting board, his cell phone rang on the countertop. He snatched it up, discovering his lawyer was calling. "Daniel," he said into the phone. "What's up?"

"Hi, Colter, sorry to call so close to dinner," he said in his gravelly voice. "I received a call from Julia's lawyer a few minutes ago. They're requesting a meeting."

"A meeting." He set the wooden spoon back down. "Did they say what they want?"

"To be honest, I'm not exactly sure," Daniel answered. "Which is the reason I'm calling. Has anything transpired between you two that I should know about?"

Colter moved to the big window in his living room, staring out at the trees dancing in the breeze. "Nothing that would warrant a meeting. I recently saw Julia at a charity event in Dallas. We were amicable."

"All right," Daniel said, and he paused, perhaps taking a note down. "Nothing happened between you two there that would upset her at all?"

"Nothing that would warrant a meeting." Colter did not feel the need to tell his lawyer about his fake engagement. "Besides, what more could she possibly want? Is she entitled to something else I'm not aware of?"

"No, she's not," Daniel said with a sigh. "I can refuse the meeting, but I suggest we have it. Meeting face-to-face is always better than over a phone call."

"All right." Colter bit the inside of his cheek to stop himself from saying things he shouldn't. "I'll be there. Send me the date and time when you've got it."

"Will do. Enjoy your night."

Colter ended the call with a curse, tossing his cell onto the counter.

"That couldn't have been a good call."

His gaze snapped up. He discovered Adeline standing in the kitchen, her arms folded over her chest. His chest squeezed at her red-rimmed eyes. "It wasn't," he said, moving to her in an instant. He opened his arms, and she walked right into them. "Julia has requested a meeting."

"Why?" she asked, wrapping her arms around his waist.

Colter pressed a kiss against her forehead, liking how

she fit so perfectly in his hold. "Your guess is as good as mine."

She gave him a good squeeze, then stepped out of his arms. "When's the meeting?"

"I don't know yet," he said. Done talking about Julia, and not wanting the focus to drift from Adeline tonight, he moved to the cabinet next to the sink and took out two plates. "Beef stroganoff okay?"

"Yes, sounds amazing," she said with a small smile, following him. "Thanks for making me dinner."

He began adding egg noodles from the strainer in the sink to her plate. "I'd ask if you were all right, but I know that's a stupid question."

She took out forks from the drawer. "It's not a stupid question, and I am all right."

"Do you want to talk about it?" he asked, scooping the sauce onto the noodles.

"If you have wine, then yes, along with a giant glass."

"That I can do," he said, handing her the plate.

He quickly fixed his own dinner, setting the plate on the kitchen table, and then grabbed a bottle of red wine from the wine rack. He poured them both a glass while she took a seat at the table. When he set a glass in front of her, he said, "So. Today was a day."

She gave a dry laugh. "It was, for certain, a day."

He joined her at the table and waited while she stared down at her meal. "I really wasn't expecting him to have a family."

"I'm sorry I never told you," he said, hating himself for it. He had figured she simply hadn't wanted to discuss Eric's family, and he hadn't wanted to add another dagger to her already-bruised heart. "I didn't realize you hadn't heard that when you learned about him."

She lifted her head, her eyes haunted, wounded. "You have nothing to apologize for," she said softly. "How could you know what I know and what I don't?" He took her hand in his, drawn into the pain seeping from her. She visibly swallowed before continuing. "From what I knew of Eric, he was an alcoholic. A terrible person. But today, that's not who I saw. I saw a family man. A father who was beloved by his family. Did you see how they looked at him? They adored him."

Colter squeezed her hand and nodded. "From what I've seen of him since I moved home, he's good to his family. It's why I was surprised when you said he was an alcoholic. That's not the man I know."

Her breath hitched and her chin trembled. "Then, if he is this great guy, why wouldn't he have tried to find me?"

Her weepy eyes felt equal to a dagger in his chest. He grabbed her chair, yanking her closer to him, cupping her face. "Whatever Eric did or did not do is on him. Not on you. You are a beautiful, brilliant, strong woman, and I have no doubt that Eric saw that today and regrets whatever terrible choices he's made along the way."

"Maybe," she said quietly, hanging her head. A tear dripped onto her bare leg. "Maybe not. But it doesn't change the fact that he should have been there in my life. For all the important moments. Even for the unimportant ones." Her voice got smaller, shoulders curling. "I wanted him there."

Colter tucked a finger under her chin, lifting her

gaze, needing to read those eyes. He wiped the tears from her face. "I'm sorry he wasn't there for you. He should have been."

"I think…" Her voice broke. "I'm honestly just sick of men disappointing me. It's like I keep trying. I keep thinking that somehow I won't be disappointed, and yet, every time I am."

"A man should never disappoint you," Colter said, adamant. "If they don't fix where they've gone wrong, they are not a man."

She heaved a long sigh that seemed to lessen the load on her shoulders. "I just keep thinking to myself, at what point should you stop caring? At what point do you say, enough is enough?"

"When someone hurts you deeply," he said immediately, cupping the side of her face. "That's when enough is enough. Neither Brock nor Eric deserved you. Don't forget that."

She leaned into his touch, her voice trembling. "But what if it is not about them? What if it's me?"

"It's not you," he stated firmly. "All this shit, Adeline, it's all on them."

Another tear slid down her rosy cheek. "How do you know?"

"Because I would rather take a knife to the heart than hurt you," he said. "That's how I know it's not you." He spread his legs and pulled her chair even closer. Holding her beautiful face in his hands, he continued, "Listen to me very carefully. Brock is a fool. Eric is a fool. Don't let their mistakes become your heartbreak."

Sweetness softened the pain in her expression. She

placed her hands over the top of his and laughed through the tears. "Has anyone told you lately how absolutely wonderful you are?"

He cleared more wetness away with his thumbs. "You just did, and that's all that matters."

"Thank you for being you. For being here. For everything, really."

He stared into her warm, honey-colored eyes, and had no idea how he was going to let her go. Life never did seem quite fair. He had regrets in his life, and he knew at this moment that not noticing her back in high school was up there with his greatest.

Somehow he needed to convince her that staying here with him was the best thing for her. And he knew now was the time to lay his heart on the line.

Leaning in near, her sugary-spicy scent engulfed him, desperate, hot need overwhelming his senses. Before his mouth met hers, he replied, "Thank *you* for being you. For being here. For everything, really."

His mouth met hers, and as he gathered her in his arms, pushing aside their plates and laying her out on the kitchen table, the last thing on his mind was their untouched meals.

An hour after they reheated their dinners in the microwave and finally ate, Adeline held her breath and sank beneath the hot bathwater in the claw-foot tub. The sounds from the house were muted, a silence she needed now more than ever. Nothing made sense. She'd talked to Nora earlier, but the only truth that remained was that she never should have visited her father. Because now she had simply added another time in her life where a man had failed her. Her happiness, her trust, her well-being all felt unhinged, ready to break in a heartbeat.

She broke the water's edge with a gasp, drawing in a breath of the warm air. She took in the bathroom with subway tiles on the walls and black shutters on the small window, the flickering candle smelling of vanilla on the vanity, desperate to relax her mind, when her cell phone rang. A quick look over the edge of the bathtub revealed her mother was calling.

She sighed and quickly dried her hands on the towel she'd left on the floor next to the tub. "Hi, Mom," she said into the phone, steeling herself for the conversation ahead.

"Hi, sweetie," Lorraine replied. "I got your message. Is everything okay?"

Her soft voice instantly made Adeline feel marginally better. "Sorry, I know it probably wasn't the best message for you to hear." Her mother had been the first one Adeline had called after she got into bed and hid under the sheets earlier. She didn't even remember what she'd said on the message, but she knew she'd been sobbing.

"The message was just fine," Mom said gently. "You sound better now."

"I ate and talked with Nora and Colter," Adeline explained. "I feel better. Raw. But better."

Mom paused. Then, "What prompted you to go see your father in the first place?"

Apparently, she hadn't explained a lot on the message. "I don't even know," she admitted, running her hand through the smooth water. "Actually, no, that's not true. I think it's because being back here has just brought a lot up. I kept thinking that maybe if I met him, I'd understand more of myself. That I'd see he was this terrible drunk, and I could finally accept that he's just a bad guy. That Brock is a bad guy. And then I could move on with my life, knowing there are bad people out there, but I don't have to change because of them."

"So, you thought meeting him would solve all your problems?"

"Yes," she admitted. Before her mother could comment, she added, "And I know that's dumb."

"It's not dumb, Adeline," her mother rebuked. "But life is rarely that easy or black-and-white." Mom hesitated again. Longer this time. When she spoke again, her voice was filled with curiosity. "Does any of this have to do with Colter?"

Of course, her mother missed nothing. "Yes. No. Maybe."

A soft laugh filled the phone line. "That sure, are you?"

Adeline lifted her hand, watching the water droplets fall from her fingers. "I'm not sure about anything, if I'm being honest. I don't even know what I'm doing. Why am I still here? Why did I play along with this fake engagement? Why did I go see my dad?" Now it was Adeline's turn to pause. The same thought that had battered her mind earlier resurfaced. "Tell me, honestly, if I was one of your patients, would you think I was losing it?"

"Absolutely not," her mother said instantly.

"Then what would you tell me?"

Her mother paused to consider. Then, "You *are* my daughter and could never be my patient, but I'll say this to you. You've been hurt, and cruelly so. What Brock did to you assaulted your trust and happiness. You must deal with that. Until you do, you'll never see things clearly. Your heart will always be tainted."

Every single word rang true in Adeline's heart.

Mom continued, "I can tell you like Colter, and that what started out as something not real has become very much real, but it would be unfair to bring anyone else into your life knowing that you're incapable of giving them all of yourself. Right now, you simply can't offer that. You can't forget the past. You can only heal after the blow you've been dealt. But pain is pain, my sweet girl. Ignore it long enough and it'll come chasing after you."

Adeline absorbed her mother's advice. "I've made all this very complicated, then?"

"What do you think?"

"Ugh." Adeline sat up, sending the water splashing in the tub. "I think I just want you to tell me what to do."

Her mother chuckled quietly. "My darling, you would never listen to me even if I did."

Knowing her mother was right on all counts, and feeling better, she said her goodbyes and ended the call with a promise to call again tomorrow before her flight.

Done with pitying herself, well aware it would get her nowhere but hiding back under the bedsheets, she got out of the tub. She quickly dried off and put on cotton pajamas before heading out of the bathroom.

She stopped short. Colter sat on her bed, her laptop in front of him. She'd done some work on the article after talking with Nora to get her mind off her unruly emotions. The tightness of his eyes told her he was reading her article. "You don't like it?" she asked, her bare feet feeling stuck to the hardwood floor.

"I like it a lot." He met her gaze. "It's good."

She winced. "Normally when someone likes something, they don't look like they've eaten a sour lemon."

He snorted a laugh, patting the spot next to him on the bed. When she sat, the mattress bouncing beneath her, he continued, "No, really, I do like it. The article is excellent. You've put my family in a good light, mentioned what the Wards stand for and made us appear to be real, hardworking people, instead of something silly, like 'Texas's sexiest bachelor.' I appreciate that."

She nibbled her lip, hating the nerves fluttering in her belly. "You sure?"

"Yes, I'm sure," he said, shutting the laptop, placing it behind him on the bed. "Truly. I liked what I read." When he rose, her breath hitched as he drew closer. "But it also reminds me that your job here is done and you're leaving tomorrow morning."

Her heart felt like it was shrinking. She wasn't ready for this conversation. "You forgot?"

"I didn't forget, but I suppose I had held out hope." He gathered her in his arms until she straddled his lap, holding her close. Pressing a kiss to the top of her head, he said, "I think somewhere in my thick head, I thought you'd stay with me rather than writing a story about me."

A swell of safety and comfort surrounded her, but a cold slice cut through, reminding her of her mother's advice. She had yet to deal with Brock and, now, the recent blow of her father. With Colter, this was all her teenage dream, a fantasy that couldn't possibly last, no matter how much she wanted it to. "But—"

"Your job. Your promotion," he offered grimly.

"Exactly," she admitted, sliding off his lap and rising, suddenly needing distance. Her heart wanted to stay in his arms, but her head, her worries and concerns, knew that to offer Colter more was unfair. She wouldn't hurt anyone like she'd been hurt. "This is...*complicated*."

"I know," he muttered, shoving his hands into the pockets of his jeans.

Emotion clogged up her throat as she fiddled with her fingers, ignoring her hands that so desperately wanted to touch him. "Besides, New York City is my home. It's my safe place. Nora is there. My mom, too."

He gave a slow nod. "I know that, too."

And yet, *and yet*, the look on his face wasn't satisfied. "Colter, asking me to stay here is like asking you to move to the city. You have your life here. With your family. It's an impossible want."

"I also know that, too." He hesitated. Rare, heady emotion swelled in his gaze. "I also know that somewhere along the way, this fake relationship has become very real to me. I know that everything in that article is written from an angle because I care deeply for you, and I know that you care about me, too."

"I do care about you," she said. And with a soft laugh, she added, "Remember, I was the one with the crush."

"Somehow we can make this work. I know I want to. Don't you?"

She never got the chance to reply before his cell

phone rang. He pulled his phone from his pocket and said into it, "Beau, what's up?"

A long pause followed. Colter's gaze locked onto Adeline's. His skin turned ashen. "When did this happen?" Another pause. "What's his condition?" And another long, horrible pause. "All right, yes, I'm on my way." He ended the call, shoving his phone into his pocket. "My dad's in the hospital."

"What?" Adeline exclaimed, rushing to his side, gripping his arm tight. "What happened?"

Colter looked shell-shocked, unmoving, unblinking. "I don't know much other than he's had a stroke."

"Oh my goodness, is he okay?" she asked, pressing a hand to his chest, feeling the thundering of his heartbeat.

Slowly, Colter shook his head. His jaw muscles clenched once. "No, no, he's not. He'd stopped breathing before the ambulance arrived at the nursing home. The medics resuscitated him, but he hasn't recovered. He's on a ventilator."

"Oh, no, Colter," Adeline gasped, coldness sinking into her bones, holding her tight. "Please. What can I do to help you?"

"Come with me," he said, his voice slow, detached. "I need you to come with me."

She took his trembling hand in his. "Yes, of course, I'm with you." She wrapped her arms around his waist, holding him close.

"Thank you," he whispered into her neck, enveloping her in his arms.

The warm, affectionate man she'd grown to know

over the past couple weeks, the man who held her now, was not the same man as he stepped back, releasing her. Fierce-eyed and jaw set, she recognized this man from the day she first saw him again in the Black Horse. She knew, as they raced to his truck, she was looking at the eldest Ward son with a legacy resting on his shoulders.

Twelve

With every step from the parking lot toward the hospital, located in a larger neighboring city to the west, Colter felt like the world was moving in slow motion around him. Adeline held his hand tight as he led her inside the hospital, the automatic doors closing behind them with a whoosh.

At the end of the hall, he spotted Beau and his mother talking to a doctor in a long white coat. As they passed by the waiting room, he saw Austin sitting in one of the chairs, playing on his iPad.

Squinting against the bright light overhead, his chest tingled as he hurried his steps. They passed a busy nursing station, followed by another corridor to the right that led to another wing of the hospital. The closer he got to his family, the more the dark-haired doctor's voice became clear.

"I'll give you time to discuss this as a family. I'll be back shortly," the fortysomething doctor said before he walked off in the opposite direction.

"Mom," Colter said.

His mother turned, burst into tears and walked straight into his open arms. He released Adeline's hand and locked his arms around his mother as she broke apart in his arms. Vaguely, he sensed Adeline and Beau were embracing, but he stayed focused on his mom. Heard every one of her cries. Felt every shake of her body. He didn't count the minutes while the strongest woman he knew sobbed in his arms. He only held her until her cries quieted, her trembling lessened and she had the strength to back away.

Keeping his arm around her, he asked gently, "What happened?"

Mom's hands shook as she wiped at the tears on her cheeks. "Today, when I went to see Dad, he seemed off. He had a lot of confusion—more than usual," she answered. "Nothing he was saying really made any sense, so the nursing staff was keeping a close eye on him."

Beau added, "The situation was challenging, because some of Dad's behavior was usual for him with his dementia. But the behavior was also warning signs of a stroke."

Mom sniffed, reaching into her purse and taking out a tissue, wiping at her nose. "The nursing staff didn't realize he was having a stroke until it was too late."

Adeline asked, "Once they realized, they rushed him here?"

"Yeah," Beau told her, his voice cracking. "But it was too late. He's unresponsive."

Colter cocked his head, that word not registering. "What do you mean, unresponsive?"

"When the paramedics arrived at the nursing home, they had to intubate him," Beau explained, shoving his hands into his pockets. "Dad's not breathing on his own right now."

Colter's knees weakened, the pale walls seemingly moving closer and closer, squeezing him tight. "There must be tests they can do—"

"He's suffered severe brain damage from the lack of oxygen," Mom said, her voice blistering. "There is no test that can fix this. The machine…"

Beau stepped forward and wrapped an arm around her and explained, "The machine is what's keeping him alive."

"Oh, Beverly," said Adeline, throwing her arms around his mother, tears in her eyes. She whispered sweet, soft comforting words.

Colter felt numb, as if he was standing there in the cold, empty hallway but also floating away. He'd been worried about himself and losing Adeline when his father had been going through this? His stomach rolled, threatening to expel his dinner all over the shiny floor.

Beau placed a hand on Colter's shoulder, squeezing tight. "It's bad, brother."

Colter nearly shook Beau's comforting hand off, but he didn't want to upset his mother more. He was the older brother. The one responsible for his family. For weeks, he'd been lost in himself, thinking *only* of himself. He should have been there for his mother, so she wasn't alone when all this happened. He should have spent more time at the nursing home. He should have been there yesterday to say goodbye. He never should have left for Seattle, leaving his father to work harder than necessary at his age. He should have taken over the ranch earlier, not chased his dreams, and maybe, his father's health wouldn't have declined so fast. He should have done a million damn things differently. He couldn't even begin to imagine what his poor mother had gone through watching her husband get intubated. "What did the doctor say?" he asked no one in particular.

Beau took Mom's hand as Adeline returned to Colter's side and answered, "Just that we need to discuss as a family what to do."

He absorbed the words, fighting even to remember how to put one foot in front of the other.

Mom asked softly, "Do you want to see him?"

"Yeah, yeah," Colter said absentmindedly.

Thoughts evaded him as he followed his family, along with Adeline, down the hallway and into a cold room on the right. The moment he saw his father, he believed two things for certain.

One, his life would never be the same after this day.

Two, he'd lost his father.

The man lying in the hospital bed, covered in a white sheet, tubes everywhere and monitoring wires leading to machines, didn't resemble the mighty cowboy Colter loved. A heart monitor beeped, breaking through the heavy silence. A nurse stood next to his father's bed, reading Grant's vitals and writing them down in a chart. He saw all this with his eyes, and yet he still couldn't believe it. He was living in a nightmare.

The nurse finally turned to them after finishing her notes and said to his mother, "I'll give y'all a moment."

"Thank you," Beau said.

When she left the room, Colter nearly sank to his knees, his breath trapped in his throat.

Adeline didn't freeze up. She walked right up to the bed and placed her hand on his father's arm. It gutted him to watch as she bowed her head and he saw her lips moving, saying a silent prayer for the man so many loved.

His father...

Sounds became muffled as she returned to his side, taking his hand in hers, but his fingers felt cold, icy.

"Colter," Beau said firmly.

Colter jerked his gaze to his brother. Beau wrinkled his brow. Right. Colter needed to do...*something*.

For as long as walking up to the hospital had felt, the walk toward Grant's hospital bed felt ten times that. His dad's arms were pale, frail in a way Colter had never seen before, his hands ashen, weak. He stared down at the fragile body and couldn't see his father anywhere in this man. And yet, *and yet*, when he took his father's hand, he felt desperate for a simple squeeze in return.

But there was no twitch of his father's fingers.

Not a single sign of life.

Colter dropped to one knee, placing his forehead on his father's hand. He even smelled different...not of earthy crops and wilderness, but of nothingness seeping through the veil of antiseptic.

He shut his eyes and said a prayer to any angel that could hear him to carry his father's spirit, wherever it lingered, to where it needed to go. *I'll take care of Mom*, he whispered in his mind, hoping his father heard him. *You don't have to worry about her or the ranch. Your legacy will live on.* Tears welled beneath his closed eyes. *You set the bar of a great man, and if I am half the man you were when I have a family, I will consider myself lucky.* He squeezed his hand one last time. *I'm going to miss you, old man. I love you, Dad.* He rose on shaky legs.

"We need to discuss what to do next," Beau said, breaking the heavy, daunting silence in the room. "The doctor is coming back to get our answer."

Keeping his father's cold hand in his, Colter glanced over his shoulder, finding his family—Adeline included—in tears. "What does the doctor need to know?" he asked.

Mom dabbed at the fallen tears on her cheeks with her tissues. "The doctor has said we can keep him on the machines and see if there is any improvement."

"Improvement for what kind of life, though?" Colter countered. He turned to face his family fully. "Who are we keeping him alive for? Him? Us?" His words felt taken right from his father's mouth. "Even if he recovers a little, what life will he lead? His Parkinson's was only getting worse. It will only become harder for him."

Mom nodded, tears rolling down her cheeks. But he knew she could never say the words that needed to be said.

Even Beau bowed his head, unable to face a decision no one wanted to make.

Adeline just cried, honest, sweet tears for his family rolling down her cheeks.

Colter itched to go to her, a desperation eating him alive, and yet...*and yet*, his father's hand... He should have been there with his father more. He should have come home sooner. He should have been there for his family. Always.

Mom's gaze roamed over her husband of forty-five years, her high school sweetheart, before she gave a long exhale. "Your father and I talked a lot about his wishes when his Parkinson's got worse, before the dementia set in. He was adamant that he did not want to be on life support."

For one last time, Colter squeezed his father's hand. He hoped his father knew that when Colter stepped into Grant's boots, he'd never step out of them. "Then we will honor his wishes," he told his family.

Adeline's eyes burned as she somberly followed Colter into the house a few hours later. Just past midnight, the house had never seemed emptier. The silence more daunting.

Grant Ward had passed away nearly immediately after the ventilator had been turned off. She had stayed next to Colter as he and Beau held their mother while they mourned the loss of such an incredible man. Adeline had waited until they began talking quietly, and then she took her leave, joining Austin out in the waiting room so he wasn't alone.

"Is Dad coming back soon?" Austin asked when she took a seat next to him.

"Yeah, buddy, soon," she replied, and he'd gone back to his game, not knowing that he'd lost his grandfather.

The family joined her not long after, and Beau had left with Austin to deliver the terrible news to his son. Adeline had remained in the waiting room while Colter assisted his mother in making arrangements with the funeral home.

Once Colter finished talking to his mother, and after they dropped her off at Beau's to stay the night with him, Colter had not said a word. Not when they arrived back at his house. Not when he got out of his truck and walked up the porch steps. Not even when they went inside.

He didn't take his boots off at the door, heading straight to his bedroom. Adeline shut the front door behind her and locked it with a sigh. She wasn't sure what she'd do if she lost her mother. Probably be a ghost, living in the world but feeling like she didn't belong. Floating through time and space, wondering exactly what she was meant to do and where she should go.

Doing the only thing that felt right at the moment, she headed for the liquor cabinet and poured him a shot of whiskey. Silence greeted her as she padded down the hallway. She found him sitting on his bed, his head bowed.

When her foot creaked against the floorboard, he glanced up. Haunted eyes met hers. "Come here," he said, patting his lap.

She closed the distance, sliding onto his lap. She offered him the drink.

"Thank you," he said, downing the shot a second later. He placed the glass on the floor next to his feet before he enveloped her in his arms, resting his face in the crook of her neck.

His muscles vibrated under her fingers. "Please tell me what I can do for you," she said.

"I'm not sure what anyone can do," he replied. "My dad is gone."

She fought her tears, wanting to stay strong for him. "I'm so sorry, Colter."

Leaning away, he heaved a long sigh. "I'm finding this hard to navigate, because the truth is, there is a small part of me that is grateful for the stroke. He is no longer suffering." He paused to tuck her hair behind her ear, following the movement with his gaze. "For years, we've watched him slowly die. Watched him fade away until I could barely recognize him. These last couple weeks only seemed to get even harder. It's been cruel."

She agreed with a slow nod. "Sometimes, death is a kindness, no matter how much it hurts."

"I think that's very much true," he said, sliding his strong hand onto her thigh. "I worry about my mother. She's been with him so long." He paused, cocking his head. "I actually don't think she's ever lived alone before. She moved right from her parents' house into our farmhouse with my dad. I'm not exactly sure what she'll do without him."

"Your mother has you, Beau and Austin. She's not alone. She'll lean on all of you."

A slow nod of agreement. Silently, he glanced down to their joined hands, and stillness fell between them.

Before now, the silence had always felt comfortable, easy. But tonight the silence felt unsteady, filled with a hundred unknowns.

When his head eventually lifted, his brows were furrowed. "I never expected you. You walked into Riggs's bar that night and shook my entire world up."

She cupped his face, dragging her fingers against the rough scruff. In a moment of sadness and death, her heart opened, revealing truths she wanted him to know. "I never expected you, either. You were my crush. My heartthrob. But you've become so much more than that."

Warmth penetrated deep into her chest at his small smile. "I want you to know that you've made me happy these past weeks. Happier than I've ever been in my life."

Why did this sound like goodbye? She shifted off his lap, kneeling between his legs to see him better. His expression was unreadable, his emotions locked up tight. "Colter—"

He pressed a finger softly against her lip. "Please, let me talk. I need to get through this."

She closed her mouth, nodding him on.

His chin dipped, his hair hanging over his brow. "Earlier tonight, when we talked, I believed that maybe, just maybe, we could somehow make this work. I would have done anything to get you to stay. But tonight is only a reminder that we are playing a game we're going to lose."

She cringed, reeling from a reality she didn't want to face. Somehow, she'd convinced herself that her feelings were easily controlled. That she could, and would, walk away. But now, nothing seemed simple anymore.

She wanted to say, "No, we can do this," because suddenly, it seemed impossible to believe she'd never see Colter or his family again. "Your family needs you," she said, reading between the lines.

"More now than ever."

"I know," she whispered.

One hand came to her nape while the other brushed across her cheek. "I know you care about me, Adeline. You don't have to tell me—I can see it."

"I do care about you," she said. "More than I think I've let myself believe."

"I'm glad for it." His gaze roamed her face, as if he were trying to memorize this moment for a lifetime. "But you have a good life in New York City. A life you've worked hard for. A promotion you deserve. You should have all your dreams come true."

"You should, too," she told him.

His eyes searched hers, his mouth pinching. "There is a truth here that I can't ignore any longer. Only pain lives here in Devil's Bluffs for you. It would be cruel of me to ask you to move here for me. Selfish in a way that I refuse to be. I will not be that type of man. Not now. Not ever."

Her breath hitched. "And I can't ask you to leave your family."

"No, you can't," he said in agreement. "And even if I wanted to, I can never leave them. Not after my father…"

Her hands ran up his thighs, the muscles beneath her touch rigid. "I'm not ready to say goodbye to you," she managed.

"I'm afraid that's exactly what you need to do."

"We don't have to do that yet," she implored, her heart leaping up in her throat. "I'll cancel my flight. I'll stay to help your mom and you. For the funeral."

All the warmth in his expression suddenly washed away, replaced by coolness. "Your flight is tomorrow morning. You should be on it."

"My God, Colter, I can stay," she said, sitting back on her heels. "I want to stay. Let me be here for you through all this."

He adamantly shook his head. Then he rose. "To draw this out is only going to hurt us both worse. I need to be with my family now. I can't think of anyone else but them."

Of course, she understood, but... "I can be there for your mother. I can help you all."

"You have a life back in New York City you have to get back to." He headed for a closet. A moment later, he came out with a full duffel bag. "You can stay the night here. Call an Uber tomorrow morning to drive you to the airport and charge the ranch."

"Colter, please wait," she said, rising, taking a step closer.

He retreated by stepping backward toward the door. "I need to be with my family. I can't think of anything else but how to help my mother find her way."

"I can go with you. Please," she begged, tears welling in her eyes. "Don't do this. Let me be there for you."

He froze in the doorway, and his shoulders lifted and fell with his long sigh. When he glanced over his shoulder, his gaze was distant, so far away from seeing her. "There is nothing here for you. We both know that. Go home, Adeline."

She wanted this. She had told him as much earlier. This could never work between them—there were too many obstacles in their way.

That made sense.

But what didn't was how everything suddenly seemed wrong when she heard the front door shut behind him.

His grandmother's ring was a sudden heavy weight on her tingling finger. She slid the ring off, leaving it on his dresser. She'd removed a ring before—Brock's ring—but *this* was worse than heartbreak. This felt like a piercing dagger to her heart.

Thirteen

Three days had passed, painfully slowly. Three days of regretting every minute that went by since Adeline had gone home to New York City. Three days of staring at his grandmother's ring, which Adeline had left on his dresser. Three days of missing *her*. He missed her laugh. Her voice. Her lush body. Even as he sat in a comfortable chair around an oblong table, in the all-glass boardroom in his lawyer's office in Dallas, his gut twisted.

Why had he told her to go?

Why hadn't he kept her close?

Why had he pushed her away?

With regrets piling on top of regrets, he gazed out the floor-to-ceiling windows to a day that matched his mood—dark and gloomy. The passing days had seemed to grow heavier, longer. Dad had been buried in the local cemetery near his parents. The funeral had brought all the townsfolk, and many out-of-towners, a show of how loved his father truly was by those who knew him best.

"Colter."

He jerked his attention back onto his lawyer next to him, suddenly reminded he wasn't alone.

Sitting across from him were Julia and her lawyer. Besides the cloying weight of Julia's perfume, she looked like the Julia he'd once loved. Simply dressed, not much makeup on her face.

"Can I have a minute alone with Colter?" Julia suddenly asked her lawyer.

Dressed in a well-fitted four-piece suit, her lawyer frowned. "I wouldn't—"

"I'll only be a moment," Julia snapped.

Her lawyer finally nodded and rose, glancing at Daniel as he did.

Daniel lifted an eyebrow at Colter in question, and Colter nodded in approval. "It's fine."

Julia reached for the pitcher of water and poured herself a glass as the lawyers left the boardroom. The same room where she'd once refused a fair deal Daniel had drawn up, instead demanding far more than she was legally allowed. Against Daniel's advice, Colter had signed her lawyer's agreement. He had wanted peace, not years spent fighting over his money.

When Daniel shut the door behind him, Julia finished her sip of water and then said, "I heard the news about your father's passing. I'm so sorry, Colter. Grant was a wonderful man."

Colter inclined his head at her sympathy. Wanting to be anywhere but there, he pushed on, "You called this meeting, Julia. Why am I here?"

A flush crept across her face. "I wanted to say that I'm sorry for everything I've done to you."

He was so stunned by her apology that it took him a moment to process that she'd said it. Still, he hesitated, unsure of her motivation. "What are you sorry for, exactly?"

"All of it," she countered, her ears turning red. "For how I handled everything after the miscarriage. For how I just let you leave without really explaining. For how I handled the divorce. For how I took more from you than I should have. For...*everything*."

Colter leaned forward, lacing his fingers together atop the table. He gave her a level look. "Is this really why you called this meeting? Just to say you were sorry? You could have done that over the phone."

"I wanted to talk to you face-to-face," she explained gently, sounding like the woman he had once loved. "I knew you wouldn't have met me if I hadn't arranged a meeting between our lawyers. I thought about calling, but I doubted you would've answered."

"I wouldn't have," he told her honestly.

She winced, hands curving around her middle. "I deserve that."

He had trouble believing his eyes. This wasn't the cold woman he'd left in Seattle.

Through the glass boardroom door, his gaze turned to Beau, who sat in the waiting room near the receptionist. His brother was frowning at him.

Colter schooled his expression to neutral as Julia said, "When I saw you with Adeline at the charity dinner, I guess it shook me. That night I realized that we've both moved on, and yet, things are still hanging there between us."

"That was your choice," he countered. "My paying alimony was not my decision."

"I know that," she said in a small voice. "Which is why I called this meeting." Her hand shook as she took another long sip of her water. She placed the glass back on the table. "When the lawyers come back in, you'll find out that I'm engaged to Bronson."

Colter lifted an eyebrow. "Do you want my congratulations?"

"No, of course not," she said, shaking her head slowly. "But I didn't want the alimony to stop because I'm getting remarried. I wanted it to stop because I, for once, actually did the right thing." Her breath hitched, chin quivering. "I've made mistakes. Big mistakes. But I want to start my life with Bronson doing things better." She paused to draw in a shaky breath. "I want you to be happy with Adeline."

He froze in his seat, the glass walls feeling like they were shattering around him. "You want me to be happy with Adeline?" he repeated.

She nodded. "I saw the way you two looked at each other and how in love you are, and, like I said, it shook me. It made me realize that I've become this person that even I don't like. It sickened me to think that you can't live your happiest life because I've got you chained to me. And I don't need you to be. When Bronson proposed, I felt…like it was time to finally move on. Time for us to let go of the past and be happy again."

Sighing dejectedly, he leaned back in his chair, seeing for the first time in a very long time the woman he'd thought he'd grow old with. "I think it's time for that, too," he told her.

"Good," she whispered. Then her voice broke. "I am sorry, Colter. For what I did to you. For how cruel I was."

Colter took in her wet eyes and inability to barely look at him. "You're fixing this now, Julia. You're doing the right thing, and that can only lead to something good."

She gave a small, sad smile before waving her lawyer back into the room.

It took a little over an hour to dissolve their original agreement. Colter kept wondering if his ex-wife would change her mind, but she never did, signing her name without a shake to her hand. He didn't hesitate in signing his.

When the meeting concluded, Julia rose, and Colter felt years of pain and shame vanish from his chest as he called, "Julia." She turned back to him, and he added, "Be happy."

She gave a genuine smile he hadn't seen in a long time. "You, too."

As they vanished down the hallway, passing by Beau, Daniel said, "That was unexpected."

Colter rose, pushing his chair back under the table. "It was." He offered his hand. "I can't thank you enough for being there for me through all this."

"We were glad to represent you and to know you,"

Daniel said, clasping Colter's hand and returning the handshake.

Colter said his final goodbyes to Daniel, and soon exited the boardroom, heading out to meet Beau.

His brother had refused to take no for an answer when he'd suggested he join Colter today. "Everything go okay?" he asked.

"It went better than okay," Colter explained, and then he gave his brother a rundown of the meeting and of Julia's change of heart.

When he finished, Beau's eyebrows were raised. "She wanted to renege on her settlement?" he asked in disbelief.

"Surprising, I know, but yes, she did," Colter answered, gesturing toward the elevator doors.

Beau followed him to the elevator. When Colter pressed the smooth button, Beau gave a low whistle. "Damn. Do you think your engagement to Adeline—"

"Yes," Colter with a laugh. "Yes, I think for some reason my moving on had Julia moving on, too."

The elevator dinged before the doors opened. Once inside, the doors shutting behind them, Beau said, "Well, I guess you owe Adeline a big thank-you."

Colter nodded, leaning against the wall as the elevator began to descend.

When the doors opened and they stepped out into the bustling main lobby of the high-rise, Beau said, "Speaking of Adeline, while I was waiting for you, scrolling through my phone, I came across something." He offered his cell phone.

Colter froze on the spot, adrenaline tingling through

his body. He read the article's headline: Texas's Sexiest Bachelor Has a Brother. And He's Even Hotter!

Colter snorted at Beau. "I take offense to that headline."

His brother barked a laugh, cupping Colter's shoulder. "Sometimes the truth hurts, brother. Not much you can do about that."

Fighting against giving Beau a rude gesture, he kept reading. First noting Adeline's name at the top. The article was familiar. He'd read the same one sitting on his bed days ago on her laptop. Only this time, he wasn't the one mentioned in the article. "Did you know she was writing this article about you?" he asked his brother.

"Yeah, she called and asked my permission."

Colter jerked his head up, flabbergasted. "And you let her?"

"Of course I did," Beau said with a slight shrug. "Like I said, I could use a little viral attention."

"Trust me, you're not going to want it," Colter countered.

"I'll be fine," Beau said gently, throwing a warm smile his way. "If it means the pressure is off you, then I can handle it."

"Beau. I can't believe you did this for me."

Beau grinned. "I'm the best, I know."

Colter couldn't laugh like he normally would. He only stared at his brother, reeling from what Adeline had done. She'd kept their time together *theirs*, just like he had told her he wanted.

His head swam, confusion making his thoughts

cloudy. He was unable to see a clear way forward. He looked to his brother. "What should I do?"

"Go after her, you idiot." Beau snorted. "Seems self-explanatory."

Colter carved his hand into his hair. "It's not that simple, Beau. There are huge obstacles between us. She'd have to give up a lot. Or I will. It's the only way it could work."

Beau cupped his shoulder again as people moved throughout the busy lobby and said, "This is very simple, Colter. Remove the obstacles."

New York had never looked bleaker as Adeline arrived at the cute two-story in Brooklyn after taking the subway. She stood beneath the streetlight, not even sure what had brought her to Brock's parents' house tonight. Only knowing she couldn't run anymore. Run from her pain. Run from her troubles. Run from how everything seemed entirely wrong since she'd left Devil's Bluffs. She missed Colter. His touch. His strength. His steadiness. She missed waking up with him every day. She missed cooking meals together and laughing over dinner. She missed every damn thing.

She even missed his grandmother's ring. Her finger feeling naked now.

Deal with Brock first, then see where you end up had been Nora's advice this morning after Adeline felt like the strands of her sanity were breaking away.

An older woman passed by her on the street, dragging a cart full of groceries, and gave a pleasant smile. Hoping the good mood continued, Adeline climbed the porch steps of the town house in the heart of Windsor Terrace, only a short walk from Prospect Park. When she reached the door with the lion's-head door knocker, she rapped briefly.

Loud footsteps moving closer sounded before the door whisked open.

Brock's light brown eyes widened. "Adeline," he exclaimed.

A stark contrast to Colter's ruggedness, Brock's brown hair was stylish, not a strand out of place. Clean-shaven, he wore dress pants and a white dress shirt rolled up at the sleeves, an expensive, flashy watch on his wrist. Brock embodied New York City.

"Hi, Brock," she said, the whoosh of a city bus speeding past the only movement. Until a pale-faced Brock glanced over his shoulder. When his gaze met hers again, he was stroking his dark eyebrow. "Stephanie is here, isn't she?"

Brock bounced from foot to foot. "I didn't know you were coming over."

"Actually, it's okay that she's here," Adeline said, a revelation to herself, too. It occurred to her then why she wasn't bothered—Brock no longer mattered. "Do you mind if I come in and talk to you?"

"Ah…" Brock didn't move an inch.

"I'm not about to lose my mind on both of you," Adeline said with a soft laugh, hoping to put him at ease. "I just want to talk to you, and Stephanie, too, if that's okay."

Suddenly, Stephanie popped her head into the hallway. She was the whole package, with her big brown eyes, designer clothes and long, straight brown hair. Adeline knew why Brock was drawn to her. Stephanie *was* stunningly beautiful. "Is it okay if we talk?" Adeline asked her.

"Um, yes," Stephanie said hesitantly. "Brock, let her in."

He stepped out of the way to let Adeline pass. She entered, leaving her shoes on as she followed Brock into the sitting room. A place she'd been so many times over the years, and where so many happy memories were made.

She stopped near the couch, not bothering to sit down. Once they sat next to each other, Brock taking Stephanie's hand, Adeline said, "I don't want to keep you long, but I think we both need closure."

Brock and Stephanie exchanged a long look. Then Brock said to her, "That's why I've been calling. To make all this better, for all of us."

She stared at their joined hands, searching for any pain from that. None came. *Colter...* "I couldn't have talked to you then, because there was a finality about it all that I wasn't ready to deal with," she admitted, laying everything she felt on the line. "But things are different now. Everything has changed. And I'm tired of running away from the things that hurt me." She paused to draw in a long breath and hastily continued, "The truth is, that cowboy I was photographed with, Colter, is someone I have grown incredibly close to, and a few days ago, his father passed away."

"I'm so sorry," Stephanie said, a hand on her chest.

The honest sympathy shining in her eyes only cemented Adeline's next steps. "After all I've been through lately, I've come to truly understand how short life is. How I never truly appreciated that. How I never really looked hard at our relationship and realized there was obviously something wrong."

Brock remained motionless, though his shoulders began hunching.

Before he could say anything, Adeline continued, "You either cheated because you're lacking something in yourself—"

Brock winced. "I—"

"Please let me finish," Adeline interjected. When he closed his mouth, she went on. "Or you cheated because you have something special with Stephanie. But you also felt like you owed me something. Maybe, in your warped way, you wanted to end things with me, but you felt bad about hurting me."

She hesitated again, glancing to their hands, their knuckles white, to collect her thoughts. Looking up into both their blank faces, she added, "Seeing that you're still together, I'm guessing that it's the latter reason you cheated on me."

Brock released a low, slow breath. "I am sorry for hurting you, Adeline."

She searched his eyes and found what she was looking for. "I actually believe that you are, in your way. But I didn't come here to give you forgiveness. You hurt me. Deeply. That won't ever change."

"Then why did you come here?" Brock asked quietly.

"To tell you that if Stephanie truly is your one true love, then I understand." Colter's kindness, his affection, his strong character, all filled her mind. "Because if Colter had come into the picture when we were together, I would have left you for him in a heartbeat."

Brock cringed, his eyes narrowing, before his expression went lax when Stephanie glanced sideways at him.

"So, I guess all that is left to say is..." She looked between Stephanie and then at Brock. "Life is too short to remain stuck in the past. I hope whatever you two were looking for, you found in each other."

Blank stares greeted her, and she smiled, her chest radiating with warmth. For the first time since she received Stephanie's call, she felt back on top of her life and free from her heartbreak. Turning on her heel, she headed for the front door.

Right when she opened it, she started, nearly walking into Brock's parents.

"Adeline," his mother exclaimed, her auburn curls bouncing atop her head. Her stumble only lasted a moment. She opened her arms in haste. "We weren't expecting you, dear."

"I made a surprise visit," Adeline explained, embracing the woman who held a special place in her heart.

Brock's father frowned beneath his thick mustache. He glanced over her shoulder at Brock and Stephanie, now entering the hallway, before addressing Adeline. "Is everything all right?"

Adeline gave a firm nod. "More than all right." She followed Brock's father's gaze, discovering Stephanie now in Brock's arms. "Brock and I got it wrong." To his mother, she added, "We did everything wrong, but somehow, it's okay that it all fell apart. We'll be happier for it in the long run." She took his teary-eyed mother back into her arms. "Just because we didn't work doesn't mean you can't keep in touch. Please do so."

His mother wiped her watery eyes. "I'd like that very much."

Feeling like a blanket of pain had suddenly been whisked off her, Adeline trotted down the porch steps, heading to the subway. Her steps felt lighter. The air felt easier to inhale.

The ping of the crosswalk sounded before Adeline hurried across the street. When she reached the curb, her cell phone rang in her purse. A quick look at the screen revealed an unknown number.

When she answered, a familiar voice she couldn't quite place asked, "Is this Adeline Harlow?"

"It is," she said, her heels clicking against the sidewalk.

A pause. "This is your father."

She froze in the middle of the sidewalk, rooted to the spot. "Eric?"

"Yes. Please don't hang up."

The air suddenly felt impossible to get into her lungs. On wobbling knees, she headed for a bench on the side of the street beneath the streetlamp. Horns honked off in the distance as she sank onto the hard wood. "I'm not hanging up" was all she could manage.

"I am so sorry for the way I handled things when you came to see me," Eric said, his voice rough. "I was taken by surprise." Another pause. Longer this time. "I'm also sorry for how I've handled everything. I made a real mess of things. But I needed you to know that when I finally got sober and got myself right, I did try to see you. By the time I went looking for you and your mother, you both had moved away. I thought, at the time, that was best. I thought you would hate me."

What he said made the world feel like it was slipping away from her. She couldn't even begin to process the meaning behind his words. But something tickled in the back of her mind. "How did you get my number?" she asked.

"Colter gave it to me," Eric explained. "Earlier today, he came by the shop... We had a chat."

"What did he say?" she asked, her heart thundering in her ears.

"He made it very clear to me that you weren't the one responsible for making this right between us. And he was right about that—this is all on me. I should have tried harder, but I was so terrified you'd hate me. I was a coward. The very worst kind." His voice blistered. "I want to make this better, Adeline. Whatever I must do—family therapy, whatever you want. I just want to get to know you. Please."

Colter's words began repeating in her mind: *There is nothing here for you. We both know that. Go home, Adeline.*

But there was something in Devil's Bluffs for her. Colter.

His actions weren't of a man pushing her away. They were of a man protecting her. A man trying to make a safe home for her.

"Adeline. Are you there?" Eric asked.

She gulped at the air, trying to steady the ground beneath her. So much had happened in, what...an hour? Her mind raced, body heated, but somehow in all that her words came easy. "I'm here, and yes."

"Yes?"

Feeling for the first time in a very long time like her life wasn't already decided for her, but she owned her next steps. She said, "Yes, I want to get to know you, too."

Fourteen

"Thanks for getting someone to watch Austin," Colter said to Beau the following afternoon, sliding onto the chair at his kitchen table next to his mother.

Leaning against the counter, arms crossed over his chest, Beau said, "No problem. Austin was glad for the playdate with his buddy."

Colter inclined his head and then studied his mother. He noted the darkness under her eyes, but he saw the strength there, too. Beverly would live on, fiercely and happily, to honor the life she'd had with Grant. To enjoy the remainder of her days appreciating the wonderful life they'd built.

She was quite the woman.

A woman who reminded him of someone else. A woman Colter refused to miss any longer. A woman who, he'd realized, had his whole heart. If losing his father had taught him anything, it was he couldn't wait for happiness to find him—he needed to chase it.

Determined to fix where he'd gone so terribly wrong, he said, "I'm sure you are wondering why I've called you over here."

Mom set her spoon down on the saucer after stirring her tea. "We're curious, yes. What's going on?"

"I've decided to take your advice," Colter told his brother. "I'm going to remove those obstacles in my way."

"Oh?" Beau asked, eyebrows lifted. "How are you going to do that?"

Colter focused on his mother's gentle eyes and heaved a sigh, dreading what came next. "I know this comes at a terrible time." He took her hand. "But…"

"You're in love with Adeline," Mom stated casually.

Colter snorted a laugh. "I'm that obvious, huh?"

"To your mother, yes," she said, patting his arm in the way she always did to let him know everything was fine. "So, I take it, you've called us here because you've decided you need to leave home and head back to the city."

He should have known his mother would have already had this all figured out. He huffed another laugh. "Why don't we just skip the part where I talk and you just tell me what I should do next?"

Mom smiled sweetly in her motherly way. "Now, that I can't do. I can only tell what you were thinking so far."

Her love was nothing he took for granted. Her kindness made him want to do better. "I'm aware my leaving now comes at a bad time, and I'm sorry to spring this on you."

"Don't be sorry," his mother replied immediately.

"Life happens. You can't hit the pause and start buttons on living your life. We lost your father, yes, but he would want us all to keep living and to be happy."

Colter agreed with a nod. "I kept thinking that I needed to be here, to do everything, to honor Dad, to do right by him. But I've come to the realization that Dad would be more disappointed if I let my chance at happiness go, to keep on in a role that is not fulfilling me and that is keeping me from Adeline."

"He would," Mom agreed.

Beau asked, "You're really thinking about moving back to the city?"

"It's the only way to have Adeline," Colter explained. He'd thought all this through. From every angle. "Her life is in New York City. It's a sacrifice I can make for her to be happy, and I will make it." At Beau's wrinkling brow, Colter pressed on, "I know taking on more work would be impossible for you. You have enough on your plate."

"It would be too much with Austin," Beau stated, carving a jerky hand through his hair.

"I know, and I wouldn't do that to you," Colter explained, running his thumb against the wood grain on the table. "Obviously, it will take more than this conversation to figure everything out, but first, I want to stay on as CEO for the ranch but lessen my workload."

Beau cocked his head. "How?"

"Hire a CFO. We'll take my salary and put it toward hiring some office staff. People to run day-to-day business on the cattle side of the ranch in my absence. And we can promote Shane to Farm Manager to run the farm, so I can return to doing what I love."

"Flying," Mom offered.

"Exactly. I miss spending more time in the air." Colter leaned back in his chair, stretching out his tight legs beneath the table. "I reached out to my old employer, and they've offered me a position with their New York City affiliate. They'll pay me well. I don't need the money I'd make here as CEO."

Mom paused to consider, taking another drink from her teacup, the floral scent infusing the air. "Okay, but what does this mean for the ranch, then?"

Colter took his mother's free hand in his, holding tight. "Like I said, I don't want to give up my position overseeing the ranch, but heading up the company was Dad's dream. He did it well. I want to honor that—keep it going in the Ward name—but it's not my dream. It's never been my dream."

Mom paused as she set her teacup back on the saucer. Then her voice cracked. "Your father didn't want either of you to give up your dreams to take over the ranch. He only wanted you to be happy. So, if moving back to the city and flying is what you want, Colter, then please, do that."

He noted her high chin but spotted the slight waver in her expression, too. He pressed his other hand atop their joined hands. "I will always be involved with the ranch, but ever since I stepped into Dad's role, I've been thinking I couldn't have it all. But I can. *We* can. We simply have to make some changes and hire the right people."

"You'll still oversee the cattle side of the ranch?" Beau asked.

"Yes," Colter replied. "If all goes as I think it will, I

can fly home for any important meetings and be in control of the direction of the farm and any big decisions. But I suspect most of my business can be done remotely." He looked to his mother, taking in her falling expression. "I also thought, if I can somehow get Adeline to forget that she just ended a relationship and get her to love me, we could split our time between the city and here, coming back on weekends and any other time we can. Not paying Julia alimony anymore would make that doable now."

Mom smiled, teary-eyed. "That would make me very happy."

"Good," Colter said, squeezing her hand. "Please take what I'm saying to heart. I don't want to walk away from the ranch. I want our land and business to stay under Ward protection, but I need to make these choices for myself."

Mom held on to him just as tight. "You should make these choices. You've done so much for your father and for me. You deserve to be happy." She watched him closely, then patted his hand. "But you're right, this isn't something that will happen overnight."

Beau's gaze was distant, thoughtful, as he scraped a hand against his jawline. "I suppose we'll have to build office space if we're hiring staff."

"I thought perhaps near the main road, where that patch of land never seems to grow a damn thing," Colter offered.

"That could work," Mom said before releasing Colter's hands to sip her tea.

Beau gave a nod of approval. "I like this idea. I think

it's good, and I think bringing in fresh eyes with new ideas could only help the ranch. I'll help wherever I can."

"Thank you," Colter said to his brother. "I know this is a big undertaking that will take some time to get resolved." To his mother, he added, "I'm still here. For you. For the ranch. No matter what."

"I know that," she said with an affectionate grin. Her gaze fell to the full duffel bag near the back door. "What's your plan now?"

"I'm flying to New York City tonight and will do my best to convince Adeline that she loves me, too."

"That girl loves you," Mom said. "We could all see it."

"Let's hope you're right" was Colter's only reply.

"Come on, then, Beau," said Mom, slowly rising from her seat. She placed her teacup in the dishwasher. "Let's get out of your brother's way."

Colter rose, and before his mother headed for the door, he embraced her. "You'd tell me the truth if this upset you, right?" he asked.

"I'm not upset, honey," she said, cupping his face, rubbing his cheeks like she had for as long as he could remember. "I adore Adeline. Nothing would make me happier than making her a part of our family." His arms tightened around her when her voice trembled. "The one thing I know that I got right in life was loving your father. When you have true love, a great love, life has meaning." She brought his face down and kissed both his cheeks. "Following your heart only leads to good things. I'm proud of you."

He hadn't thought he needed his mom's approval, but

a heavy weight on his shoulders eased with her support. "Thank you."

Beau took Colter into a rough hug. Then he let go and said, "Just don't say something stupid and mess it all up."

"I'll try not to." Colter snorted, following them to the front door.

Outside on the porch, Beau trotted down the steps, waiting at the bottom to hold Mom's hand as she walked down, when Mom suddenly stopped.

"Oh, I forgot to mention," she said, glancing at Colter. "Do you still have your grandmother's ring?"

"Yeah, of course," Colter replied. "Want me to get it?"

"Hmm." Mom's smile slowly built. "I think it's best if you keep it."

Seated in the back seat of the Uber, Adeline said into her phone to Nora, "I think I'm going to puke." Ever since she got off the phone with her father last night, she'd been on autopilot.

She'd used a good chunk of her savings to take a private flight, using the same company that Colter had worked with before, to get to Dallas fast. Then an Uber got her the rest of the way, and she'd been on the phone with Nora ever since.

The Uber driver glanced in horror at her in the rear-view mirror. She waved him off. "Don't worry, I won't puke in your car."

With a relieved look, he glanced back at the road.

"That poor driver," Nora said with a laugh. "And, dude, let's be real here. You have faced Brock and your father and have come out stronger and happier for it.

Those things were both hard as hell. What you have with Colter is easy. This is good. You deserve this. Relax."

"I do deserve this, don't I?"

"Yes, you do. So stop almost puking, lift up your beautiful chin and go and get your cowboy."

Adeline smiled —a real smile that seemed to feel so honest now that she was back in Devil's Bluffs. New York had felt different when she'd gone back. Like nothing made sense there anymore. Here, everything seemed... *right*.

The Uber driver turned into the driveway, and Adeline spotted Beau's truck driving away from Colter's house and down the road. Her stomach fluttered with butterflies as she said, "We're here. I need to go."

"Call me after. Good luck," Nora said.

"I will. Love you."

"Love you, too."

Adeline ended the call and then asked the Uber driver, "Can you please go faster?"

The driver hit the gas, speeding up the driveway, and she tapped her fingers against her twitchy leg. Until she saw Colter's truck in the driveway. He was there...and she was... Well, she hadn't quite figured that part out yet.

When they reached the porch, the car's tires skidded to a halt. "Thank you," Adeline said, taking her overnight bag with her as she exited the Uber.

"Enjoy your evening, miss," the driver said.

She slammed the door shut, and as he drove off down the driveway, she walked closer to the house. Until she stopped, pressing her hand against her chest, convinced she was having heart palpitations. Through the big front window, Colter was heading toward the back door, carrying a duffel bag.

"Are you…leaving…" She threw the strap of her bag over her shoulder and ran as fast as she could muster around the house, spotting him heading toward his helicopter.

Breathless, she yelled, "Where are you going?"

He stiffened. Then he glanced over his shoulder. Like he couldn't believe she was standing there, he dropped his bag and moved closer, but not as close as she wanted him. Not nearly close enough. The distance between them felt cold…empty.

"Where are you going?" she repeated.

"To the city," he said, statue-still. "To you."

"You hate the city."

"I love you more."

All the guards around her heart shattered. "You love me?"

"Madly." He took a step toward her, warming the air between them. "Deeply." And another step. Until he stood directly in front of her. "I am in love with you, Adeline, and I don't want to live without you."

Her breath hitched. Tears welled in her eyes. "I love you, too."

"Now *that* is exactly what I wanted to hear." He charged forward and gathered her in his arms as she wrapped her thighs around his legs.

The dry air brushed across her as his mouth met hers, and she gave everything she had to him. She wasn't thinking hesitation or lust—she was only thinking about the rightness of the moment. How it didn't matter if everything made sense between them. Somehow, someway, this was going to all work out, because they were meant to be together.

She vaguely felt him moving, but his sizzling kisses never broke away. Not until he reached the back door to open it and kicked it shut behind them. While he carried her to the bedroom, she placed butterfly kisses on his mouth, his jaw, his neck, where she nipped a little.

He groaned deep, then tossed her on the mattress. She laughed, bouncing against it, but stopped when he hovered over her. Intensity stared back at her. "How are you here?"

"Well, Eric called," she told him, cupping his handsome face, scraping her fingers against the scruff. "He told me what you said to him. I guess I realized that while it is scary for me to stay in Devil's Bluffs, and my life is very uncertain here, there is also nowhere else I'd rather be."

He slowly shook his head, pulling her up to sitting. He went down to one knee in front of her. "I've already talked to my family. We're hiring staff to handle the cattle portion of the farm. I'm moving to New York City."

"I mean, you are more than welcome to move there if you want," she said with a slight shrug. "But earlier today, my boss and I came to an arrangement that I would freelance for her. I also accepted the position as editor for the *Devil's Bluffs Chronicle*, since Waylon is retiring."

His eyes widened. "You're moving here?"

"No, I'm not moving here," she corrected. "I *moved* here. Tonight." Of course, then she realized she'd spoken too soon. "I'll need to go back to New York City to pack up all my stuff and ship it here. Then sell my condo. But my heart…it lives here, in Devil's Bluffs."

"With me?"

She cupped his face again. "With you."

"Adeline," Colter murmured, resting his forehead against hers. "I was ready to uproot my whole life, and here you are offering me everything. Changing everything. Like you did from the first night I saw you at the bar."

"Changing everything for the better," she said. "I know why my mom left here, why she needed to move away. But this is my home. It's always been my home. And I want to get to know Eric. I want to see where all this takes me."

"I'll be right at your side to do that, too."

"I know," she said, her chest swelling with possibilities. "I thought, maybe, we could go to New York City on the weekends sometimes to visit Nora and my mother."

"We can go as often as you want," he said, adamant. "Do whatever you want."

She laughed, stroking his face. "Better be careful. You're offering me the world, and I just might take you up on it."

"I will give you everything," he said. "And then I will give you even more. You made me believe in love again when I thought that was impossible."

She felt breathless, weightless and everything in between as she said, "You made me fall in love with you after the greatest betrayal. Though, to think on it, maybe I've always loved you."

Emotion-packed eyes held hers as his hand lowered

to his pocket, and then he put his grandmother's ring on her knee. "I took too long to notice you, but I won't ever not see you again. This ring never should have come off your finger. What do you say, New York—will you marry me for real?"

Her finger tingled as he slid the ring back onto her hand. What had been missing was now whole again. "Yes, Colter, absolutely, yes. I'll marry you."

Intensity and happiness and so many other things she could never name flashed through his expression as he sealed his mouth across hers. He swept her away in a kiss that was more that affection, it was a promise, one she felt weave around her.

Frantically, he removed her clothing, piece by piece, and she removed his until there was nothing between them. Only skin against skin, and all the love between them. He backed away only once, to sheathe himself in a condom, before his kiss turned hot and wicked as he laid her out on the bed.

"Not tonight," she told him. "Tonight, I want to have you." She squirmed out from under him until he allowed her to push him onto his back. Staring down at the man who'd stolen her heart so early in her life, and then again when she wasn't looking for love at all, she straddled his waist and gazed upon him. His handsome face. His mouthwatering, muscular physique. "This might end badly for me, you know," she said, wiggling her hips to find the tip of him.

"How is that?" He groaned as she sank down on him, gripping her hips tight.

She brushed her puckered nipples against his chest.

"I'm going to be the most hated woman in Devil's Bluffs." He moaned, his eyes shutting as she moved slowly, taking him in, inch by inch. "I have taken Texas's sexiest bachelor off the market...for real."

"Let them be jealous." He lifted his head off the bed, capturing her mouth. His hands roamed every inch of her until he cupped her breasts, massaging them.

She couldn't think as sensation overloaded her. Touched by him, filled by him, she couldn't talk anymore. Not as she pressed her hands on his chest and shifted against him, back and forth, overwhelmed by how amazingly he stretched her. How deep he was. How his hands claimed her. How his touch invaded deep into her heart.

Pleasure began blinding her as she tipped her head back, bouncing on him, his gripping hands helping her move faster, harder until she found a rhythm that brought the intensity they both needed. His groans followed the sound of skin slapping, mirrored by her own moans, the scent of their sex driving her higher.

She moved harder, faster yet, needing *more*.

Then she was staring into smoldering, half-lidded eyes as he fisted her hair, bringing her mouth down to his. He kissed her with a passion she hadn't known before. A statement no man had ever placed on her body.

She knew, with absolute certainty, that from this night on, he was hers and she was his.

Like he knew it, too, he growled against her mouth, an animalistic sound that spoke to every feminine bit of her soul. With his free hand, he grabbed a fistful of her bottom and thrust up from below.

Just like that, time stopped clicking.

And they hung, on the edge, staring into each other's souls, until their love blew their worlds apart.

Fifteen

Standing in the kitchen, listening to Blake Shelton on the radio, Adeline placed the drying towel back onto the stove's rack. One month had gone by since the night Colter slid his grandmother's ring back onto her finger. One night that had changed everything for the better. The first couple weeks had been a hectic mess and left Adeline busier than she had ever imagined possible. With the help of her mother and Nora, they'd packed up her condo in three days and shipped all her belongings to Devil's Bluffs.

Now Colter's house didn't feel like just his house anymore. Her stuff was all there, too. He'd gladly taken some of his things away so she could hang her favorite pieces of art and decorate the space to put her touches on things, too. Devil's Bluffs finally felt like home.

Her home.

She'd started the process of taking over for Waylon, but his retirement was a few months off, so she had time to get settled. And she had already written a few freelance pieces for the blog. But it wasn't only her life settling—Colter's was as well. Every day when he came home from flying the helicopter, he arrived with a big smile. The same smile that had been there ever since they'd hired a CFO and three other employees to run the business side of the Devil's Bluffs Ranch, plus promoted Shane.

Everything had somehow settled into place, and life was...*good*.

As Colter finished drying a pot, Adeline focused on the one part of her life that was the hardest. She smiled at Nora on FaceTime as her best friend complained about the current employer who contracted her. "She can't be that bad," Adeline said.

Nora gaped. "She is worse than you could probably imagine. I have never met a person so into herself in my life. It's unbelievable. Seriously, she can talk about herself for an hour straight. I timed it."

"An hour, for real?"

"Yes," Nora exclaimed. "An hour. Then, no matter what anyone is talking about, somehow we end up talking about her again. She's got all these conspiracy theories she believes. When someone tries to disagree, she is horrible to them. Honestly, I think she might be the devil."

Behind her, Colter chuckled. Which abruptly ended as the front door burst open.

Beau bolted inside, slamming the door shut. "You

owe me," he growled. When he turned around to lean against the door, his face was bright red, his nostrils flaring from obvious exertion. "You owe me so bad."

Colter relaxed with a laugh, hanging the drying cloth next to Adeline's. "I told you that you never should have gone viral on purpose."

"I had no idea it would be this bad." Beau glared. "You *both* owe me. This is crazy."

Nora snorted a laugh.

Reminded that her best friend was still on FaceTime, Adeline said, "I'm actually really glad you're here, Beau," she told her future brother-in-law. "Since you're Colter's best man for the wedding—" they were in the planning stages of a small, personal ceremony "—and Nora's my maid of honor, you two should probably meet." She turned her phone around, and Beau's brows furrowed.

Eyes narrowed, he closed the distance and snatched the phone away. "What was that laugh about?" he asked Nora.

Adeline nibbled her lip, holding in her laughter now. If Beau thought Nora would back down when pressed, he was dead wrong.

As expected, Nora said, "My snort laugh, you mean?"

"Yeah, *that*." Beau's chest heaved.

Nora didn't hesitate for a single moment. "Because I find what you said hilarious. Seriously, you have available women chasing after you and you're unhappy about this. What is wrong with you?"

Beau lifted his brows. "What would you do if you were in my position?"

"I'd enjoy the ride," Nora said, and Adeline knew

she meant that. Nora was wild and free and never settled down. Adeline couldn't imagine her ever being in a serious relationship. "Free dinners. Coffee dates. Fun nights out. Oh, what torture you must be enduring."

Beau's nostrils flared again. "Then you make a photograph of yourself go viral."

"I can't," Nora said dryly. "I'm not nearly as hot as you."

One eyebrow slowly lifted. A beat passed between them. As though, for the first time, Beau had actually gotten a good look at her. "The problem here is it's not only women hunting me down, it's reporters." He finally handed the cell phone to Adeline, and said to Colter, "I want to get out of town for a while."

"It's that bad?" Colter asked.

Beau nodded. "Can Austin stay with you two for a couple weeks? You'll have to take him to school and handle lunches and his baseball games, but I can't allow him to deal with this nonsense. He can't understand why there's people always following us."

Colter sidled next to Adeline, leaning against the island. "Yeah, of course he can stay. Where are you going?"

Beau gestured at Adeline's cell phone. "I'll let you know later."

Adeline withheld her laughter.

"Just being a voice of reason," Nora piped up. "But reporters never back down unless given a reason to."

"They won't have a choice," Beau spat. "I'm leaving tonight."

Nora was grinning. Adeline fought her smile. Her best friend was the worst kind of instigator.

"I wouldn't recommend that," Nora offered.

"Why is that?" Beau glared at the phone.

"Because they'll hunt you down wherever you go," Nora said dryly. Then she shrugged, "At least that's what I'd do." And being one of the best researchers Adeline knew, Nora would find him, too. She uncovered buried secrets no one else could find.

Beau closed the distance again and held out his hand for the phone. Once Adeline handed it to him, he said to Nora, "They will never find me."

Nora grinned. "They will, believe me. You should rethink your strategy."

He made a noise in the back of his throat.

"Are you always this grumpy?" she asked.

Beau frowned at the phone and harrumphed before he handed Adeline the device and left, slamming the front door behind him.

"That went well," Adeline said, lifting the phone back to her face. "I can tell already you two are going to be the best of friends."

"Men are silly," Nora said.

"Man here," Colter called.

"You're Adeline's man. That's different," Nora said with a sheepish smile. "I need to get going, but keep all the wedding plans coming. I'm loving everything you're sending me. Are you still planning on coming to New York City this weekend to see your mom?"

"That's the plan," Adeline answered.

"Great," Nora replied. "Then let's make sure we do something fun on the town. Colter needs to get some city nightlife into him."

"I'm not sure that sounds appealing," Colter muttered.

Nora either didn't hear him or wasn't paying attention, since she added, "All right, you two, lots of love. Toodles."

"Love you back." Adeline sighed when the screen went black. "That was a disaster," she said to Colter.

"Not a total disaster," Colter said, tugging her close, wrapping her in the warmth of his hold. "Beau seemed to not mind Nora."

"You cannot be serious," she gasped. "I've never seen him be so snippy with anyone."

Colter pressed a kiss on her forehead before he shrugged. "He's obviously in a mood over being hounded by reporters and available women, but he also backed down. Beau never backs down. Trust me, I know, he's been the annoying younger brother most of my life."

Adeline considered and then shook her head slowly. "Nora's right—men are silly."

He tapped her nose, grinning. "Women make us that way." Holding her tight around the waist, he watched her a moment, his gaze narrowing on her mouth, and only then did she realize she was nibbling her lip. "What's wrong?" he asked.

"Maybe we should hold off on planning the wedding until Beau is back and everything has calmed down."

"That is a hard no from me," Colter countered, caging her between him and the kitchen counter with his arms braced on either side of her. "Plan away—" he dropped his mouth close to hers "—because I'm already growing impatient."

"Impatient for what?" she asked, running her hands up his strong arms, flexing beneath her touch.

He brushed his lips against hers. "For you to be my wife."

She slid her hands up his squared chest. "Is that all you want?" she rasped.

"Oh, I want much more than that." He grinned, weakening her knees in a way she hoped he'd always weaken them.

"Good—you are my crush, after all." She angled her head back, leaning up, offering herself.

"Not your crush," he corrected, brushing his lips across hers. "I am yours and only *yours*."

"And I am irrevocably yours." She smiled against his lips. "I love you, Colter."

"Love you back, New York."

* * * * *

HARLEQUIN
PLUS

Announcing a **BRAND-NEW**
multimedia subscription service
for romance fans like you!

Read, Watch and Play.

Experience the easiest way to get
the romance content you crave.

Start your **FREE 7 DAY TRIAL** at
<u>www.harlequinplus.com/freetrial</u>.